YOUNG VIKINGS
AND THE QUEST FOR
ASGARD

DR. J. SCOTT HARDIN &
DR. SUSAN A. HARDIN

CONTENTS

PROLOGUE

In an era called the Middle Ages, the Norsemen, also known as Vikings, set up settlements across the Northern Atlantic. The Vikings made a name for themselves as fearless and resilient warriors as they traveled the seas in search of land and resources. Stories of their vast journeys were passed down for generations. Such tales included gods in the heavens, trolls from the undergrounds, and giant blue whales of the high seas. During the late Middle Ages, the Vikings' settlements and commerce thrived. They became excellent fishermen, farmers, and merchants, trading goods and services with neighboring communities. The word "Viking" is used to describe a lifestyle. A lifestyle that exhibits the traditions and customs of the Viking culture, their way of living, their devotion and loyalty to family and countrymen, and a civilization that battled, conquered, and survived.

CHAPTER I

LEGENDS, MYTHS, AND MONSTERS

The battle has been raging for days, or at least it feels so...really, it has only been a matter of hours. Bodies of men, trolls, goblins, ogres, and hobgoblins litter the ground as far as the eye can see. Three brave Vikings find themselves trapped in the tower of an ancient and crumbling castle. Jotur, Tredge, and Yves, the only Vikings left to fight, discover they are in a desperate situation. They are isolated, outnumbered, and surrounded. The tower offers a moment of respite and safety, but they know they cannot stay there.

"We should climb to the top of the tower and signal for help," Tredge says, pointing upward.

"...Or we could use our bows to clear a path of escape," Yves suggests.

Jotur interjects, "We don't have enough arrows, and there is no one left to help us. We will need to wait until the ogres and trolls forget about us, and we can just slip past them while they sleep."

"I don't think they'll forget about us that fast!" Tredge says.

"No, you're right. They aren't going to fall asleep for a long time, and even though trolls aren't the brightest, I don't think they will just forget about us anytime soon," Yves replies. "We have to fight."

"I know! We should start a fire, let it spread out around the tower, and follow it with swords and spears!" Tredge says as he holds up his sword, ready to fight. "I can build a tinder nest and start the fire," Tredge looks at them for approval.

They imagine the course of the outcome for each suggestion. Finally, the three decide simply to charge forth from the tower entrance and fight with all their might, hoping for the best. Drawing their swords, holding up their shields, and praying to the gods, the Vikings set forth to fight. Suddenly and without a signal between them, as if their minds were one, they burst forth through the doorway of the tower. Yves leaps onto the back of the first ogre he sees and begins to attack it with his sword.

"Take that, you ugly best!" he says as he begins to take him down. It bellows with a loud, long wail.

"Aaghhh!" Jotur lunges with her sword in front of her at the second ogre. Startled by her approach, it retreats a few steps back. Tredge grabs a nearby troll by the ears. It jerks and tries to swing him away, but he holds on tight for dear life. The three warriors are willing to fight until the end, though they are far outnumbered.

Suddenly, a voice calls out of nowhere, "Jotur, Tredge, Yves! It is time for supper! And you better not let your father see you aggravating those pigs and cow." As the young Vikings pause from the battle to listen, the tower and castle of their imagination slowly fade into a silo and barn of reality. The ogres and trolls change back into their beloved farm animals, the pigs and cow, who seemingly ignore the children attacking them.

"Yes, mam," the three warrior children chime in chorus together.

The children run into the house where their mother, Elsa, stood. Their mother, a beautiful redhead with soft curls dangling from her loosely tied bun, is not a fighter. The children often laugh when she tries to battle with them and can barely hold a sword upright. She is not your usual Viking but rather the peacemaker of the family, the thread that holds them all together. Elsa would often settle arguments or "theological debates," as Jotur and Yves like to call them. The children rush past her to quickly wash up for dinner, hungry from their big battle. They love family supper time.

The Jurgenson Family

The children enter the kitchen, and Jotur, the only daughter and the eldest, quickly helps her mother place the food on the table. Jotur is to turn seventeen years old upon the new moon. She is strong and healthy, has freckles her dad calls "kisses" on her nose and cheeks, and wears her long reddish blonde hair down in two braids on each side of her shoulders, like many of the Viking women. Unlike her mother, she is skillful with a bow and very dexterous with a short sword. Her father, Sigvard Jurgenson, is already sitting at the table and is growing impatient.

"Did ya'll win your battle today?" he asks, knowing exactly what they had been up to in the fields. Sigvard is a strong Norman Viking with a legacy going back centuries. Per tradition, he has shaved the back half of his head entirely, as most of the Viking men have done from their village.

"Yes, sir!" Tredge exclaims in excitement at his father's question. "We were surrounded by trolls and ogres and goblins and…." His dad laughs out loud at Tredge's expressions. Tredge is the youngest of the three, having just turned age nine, and is short and stout. He loves to make his family laugh and thinks of it as his job, which he takes seriously.

"Tredge," his mother interrupts, "Prayers first."

The family prays to the gods of Asgard for their rustic seaside village, known as Svalbard. They plead for the fish to keep biting and for peace and prosperity to continue. Svalbard was not always so amicable, but the wars of their elders had all but faded, and they enjoyed living in a time of peace. The sagas of heroes and mythical legends have now become stories often told at bedtime. The children are hungry and eat without much conversation until Sigvard puts down his fork and scoots his chair back, finished.

"How is your carving coming along?" their dad asks. Tredge is very agile with his hands and adept at carving small creations. He often sculpts creatures in small pieces of wood he finds on his walks through the fields.

"I worked on it this morning," Tredge responds. "You can't see it until it is finished!" His favorite to carve are usually figures of beasts and monsters, but his latest challenge is the figurehead on his father's boat. It is going to be a magnificent dragon's head.

"That was very good, Elsa," Sigvard says, complimenting her.

"I'm glad you enjoyed it," she says, pleased. "The garden has blessed us this season," she adds.

"Father, could you please tell us a story?" Tredge quickly takes the opportunity to ask. He is always anxious to hear about the Vikings' sailing adventures and battles conquering the world.

"Yeah, father please?" Yves asks too. Yves looks lanky yet is very strong and is developing into a young Viking man. He is fourteen and named after his uncle, a great Viking warrior. He enjoys sailing with his father and often accompanies him on fishing trips in which his dad would tell many tales of the gods and war. He has been taught the traditional skills of a bow and sword, but his expertise lies more with his cleverness and book smarts. He loves to read and can often be found on the rooftop of the barn or in the haystacks, reading a story about the adventures of the gods.

"Yes, please tell us one," Jotur agrees.

Sigvard takes a deep breath and thinks about what story he could tell his children tonight. Tredge sits up straight, ready to listen. His dad begins.

"Today, the Vikings are farmers and fishermen, but long ago, they were fighters, conquers. In the cold and desolate land of Norway, our neighboring villages were not as friendly as they are today. The Vikings had enemies and predators. Though we have earned great respect for our neighboring countrymen, it has not always been so. Before we lived and traded in peace, we were enemies. It was a time of poachers, bandits, and, worse, mythical creatures such as trolls and others unseen." Sigvard pauses for effect and takes a sip of his drink, then continues.

"...As in tradition, each Viking is trained to fight the Viking way, as great warriors, ready to protect their village and their families at a moment's notice," he says as Tredge's eyes open wide at the sheer mention of trolls and mythical creatures.

Sigvard changes the subject to tease him. "And did you know there are two types of ships the Vikings use? One is the warship called a Langskip, and the other is a merchant ship called a Knorr. The warship is more narrow and longer, powered by oars and sails; unlike the Knorr, it is built for speed." But, of course, he knows Tredge already knows all this.

"We know, we know! Get to the mythical creatures, father!" Tredge exclaims.

"Patience, my son," Elsa reminds him gently. "He will get there."

"Mythical creatures, you ask?" Sigvard teases, amusing himself.

"Yes!" exclaims Tredge excitedly.

"Okay, okay," says Sigvard. "Now, where was I? Oh, yes…so we live in the Midgard region, which is connected to Asgard by a great rainbow bridge called Bifrost. We can often see Bifrost in the northern sky, but no one knows how to reach it. We must die in battle as great warriors to cross the rainbow bridge."

Yves interrupts, "But if we aren't fighting and in a time of peace, can we reach Asgard?" he asks.

"No questions," his father replies, not really knowing the answer himself, for it is only a story. Sigvard continues. "Our great ancestors, for example, were taken by Valkyries to the great hall of Asgard. The Valkyries are beautiful warrior women with long golden hair who ride on winged horses adorned with shiny armor, looking fearsome and strong. They swoop down onto the battlefields choosing gallant warriors to serve in Odin's army."

"Until the day of Ragnorak," Yves chimes in.

"Yes, until the end of time," Sigvard concurs.

Jotur, Yves, and Tredge are intrigued by the legends and love hearing these stories from their father. Even though Tredge, only nine, is familiar with the legends, Yves and Jotur know them by heart. When they were younger, they would go into the village just to hear the elders recount the tales of the gods. They would listen to stories of the hammer called Mjollnir, the flaring bridge to Asgard, and the realms of elves and dwarfs. Yves read extensively in The Great Hall, where the scrolls and archives of their forefathers were kept. Each god and goddess had their own unique qualities representing at least one attribute of the mortal spirit, such as morality, heroism, integrity, and so forth. And Yves knew them all. This evening's story focuses on the infamous god Loki, the god of mischief. They knew the story well but still listened to their father late into the evening.

The Old Norse Festival

The following day Tredge arises early in excitement for the fall festival. The Old Norse festival, a weeklong event, is full of friendly games of combat and contest for all ages, men, women, and children.

"What are you doing up so early," his dad asks, seeing Tredge heading towards the front door.

"Only two days left to finish my shield," he yells back, not stopping but heading out the door. "I want to get an early start." The local townsmen compete in sword fights, handy work with an axe, horsemanship, and archery, and the children compete in shield design.

"Wait, come back here," his mother calls out from the kitchen. "Your father and I are going to run into the village this morning."

"Can I come, please?" Tredge asks, always enjoying a trip into town, but today the villagers were up earlier than usual, finishing up their arts and crafts for selling and preparing for the competitions.

"Many will be sitting up today, and I want to watch," Tredge begs his mother. "Please!"

"No, you have chores, remember?" his mother reminds him, "...and you have to be all caught up because next week we won't be able to get anything done with the festival going on."

Tredge turns to his dad, who just walked into the room. "Please, dad? I won't get into any trouble." Elsa gives Sigvard a look for him not to cave.

"No, your mother is right. There will be plenty of time for you to get into trouble next week. Today I need to get some supplies for you to complete your shield so you can enter it in the contest." Sigvard reaches for his coat. "Are you ready to go?" he asks his wife. "I have some fish to trade, and I want them to be fresh."

"I need to gather some vegetables from the garden first, so just go ahead, and I can meet you at the market at lunchtime," she replies.

Once Sigvard gives the final "No" to Tredge, his attention drifts, and he begins to wonder about the various swords and shields they will have on display this year.

"Ogres! Why is it always ogres?" he asks himself aloud as he leaps forward, lunging with his imaginary sword. He turns around and takes off toward the front door again. "I'll get you this time!" he shouts.

"Chores!" his mother calls out, reminding him once again.

"Oh, yeah," Tredge replies, disappointed, "I forgot."

***

The parents leave their three young Vikings at home while they head into the village. The rules of being left alone were simple, "Do your chores, and Jotur is in charge." The children quickly finished their usual morning chores of feeding the animals and cleaning the stalls and were now working inside the house. Yves sits quietly on the floor making new ropes for the crossties in the barn, a responsibility he says to have finished weeks ago. Tredge, never far from his brother's side, is cleaning their dad's sword and shield for the upcoming competitions. Yves tries not to correct Tredge, ignoring the mess he is making with the oil soap, but he does so while biting his tongue. As yet another drop of oil falls to the floor, Yves watches from the corner of his eye. He tries hard to ignore it and focuses on his ropes, trying not to miss a loop; however, his mind is distracted. Yves tries to think of something else as he braids the cords. He envisions the sight of his father fighting in last year's competition, picturing him with his shield and sword. Yves had watched his father train many nights when he was supposed to be in bed fast asleep. He would sneak out and watch between the fence posts. Occasionally, after supper, his dad would let him spar with him, but he thought this was more for his benefit than his dad's. As he continues to daydream, he doesn't realize he has stopped working and is staring straight ahead with a big smile on his face. His sister startles him back to the present moment.

"Yves!" Jotur interrupts his vision of victory. "You will never finish those ties if you don't stop daydreaming and wipe that goofy grin off your face." Tredge laughs at her scolding Yves. He's usually the one getting in trouble.

"And your pies, they're going to burn if you don't stop worrying about others and pay attention to your own doings," Yves responds smugly as he lifts his nose in the air and takes a big whiff. An aroma has filled the room of buttery, crisp baked crust and ripe apples, perfect at the moment but easily turned disastrous if not carefully watched.

"Oh, no, not my pies! Those are for the festival," Jotur says as she immediately runs off toward the oven. The focus is now off Yves. He looks at Tredge, and they both laugh out loud.

BONGGGG! Suddenly, they hear a thunderous clanging sound that interrupts their laughter. Immediately they stop laughing, and the house falls silent as the two brothers freeze in their tracks, neither eager to move.

Jotur, also hearing the noise, looks up from the oven. "The BELL?" she says with distress in her voice. The boys look at her as if she is supposed to know what is happening. Tredge, having never heard the bell before, is excited for a fleeting moment, thinking it is to signify the beginning of the festival, but when he sees Jotur's face, he knows she thinks otherwise.

"What's that?" Tredge questions. He knew the bell was there, but he had never given it much thought.

"It is the town's bell," Jotur says. "The warning bell."

"The warning bell?" Yves repeats. "So dramatic!" Yves says, teasing her. He often thinks she is overreacting. "It only rang once. It was probably an accident or test or something."

Jotur walks over to Tredge and stands by him like a protective mother. She thinks hearing the bell is a serious matter, unlike her brother Yves. Jotur bends down next to Tredge and places her hand on his shoulders.

"Tredge, we need to be prepared," she says to him. "You need to take cover in the storage bin and hide."

'*Wow, she looks just like mom doing that,*' Tredge thinks to himself, not paying attention to her words of heed.

"Tredge!" she raises her voice this time. "Contrary to your brother's belief, this is serious. It's the town's warning bell." This time, her voice cracks with emotion when she speaks, and he knows she is earnest. '*A warning,*' she thinks to herself. '*Now, what could they possibly be warning us about?*'

"Jotur, the bell, though an alarming sound, just startled us. The surprise of the loud clanging came as a shock to our ears, but there is nothing to be concerned about," Yves says, trying to calm her down. "Perhaps mom and dad forgot to tell us they are testing it today."

"But it has been silent for so long," she reminds him, "…and they've never tested it before."

"Yeah, just my point. None of us knew what it sounded like," Yves claims.

"Yeah, LOUD!" Tredge says, showing his support for his brother's theory.

"You are probably right," she sighs.

"Both probably right," Tredge corrects her.

"Yes, both probably right," she says, rolling her eyes. Yves gives her his youthful and charming smile, and she begins to drop her guard.

"So what is this warning bell? I didn't even know we had a bell," Tredge asks, confused why he didn't know about it, and they did.

"Tredge, do you know The Thor Tower at the marketplace?" Yves asks. The hall was located in the epicenter of the village.

"Yeah, it's where the market is," Tredge answers. "How could I not know that? The tower is the tallest building in the village, and it's where you hang out all the time reading...boring!"

"Well, you know how Thor has an enchanted hammer called Mjollnir," Yves tells him, "which was made by the dwarfs?"

"Yeah, of course, I know the hammer," Tredge answers. "What do you think? I'm a baby?"

"Well, in order to wield the mighty Mjollnir, Thor wears a belt of strength," Yves continues.

"...And iron gloves," Tredge adds. "Hey, aren't those a little heavy to be wearing around?" Tredge asks, holding up his hands and imagining having heavy gloves on.

"I don't know; I guess it's easy because he's a god," Yves says, having never given it much thought before.

"Do you know who his father is?" Yves asks him.

"Yeah, Odin, the leader of the gods!" Tredge replies, proud to show off some of his own knowledge of the legends.

"...And Odin sits on a throne from which he can see the entire world he created with his brothers and has many wonderful and magical treasures. Among them are two wolves that serve him and two ravens which bring him news from around the world, but the most magnificent is his horse, an eight-legged horse who is the fastest and most gallant of all the horses of the world."

"Wow!" Tredge didn't know that. "Think how fast I could run if I had eight legs!"

"We'd never be able to catch you!" Yves laughs, knowing he would enjoy that little fact.

"…And did you know if you start from the Thor Tower in the center of the village and walk south or north toward the town's walls, it is exactly the same distance until you reach either side?" Jotur adds, annoyed with Yves' distractions and for not taking the bell seriously. "See, we all know things, now focus, what could the bell mean? Did you hear anyone talking about ringing it for the festival this week?" Jotur asks, looking right at Yves, wanting his attention.

Tredge, still trying to figure out how she measured the distance from the tower to the wall, has to ask, "How do you know that? Did you try it? Walk it out? Can we try it?"

"Ugh, I just know," she tells him frustratedly, but she doesn't really know if it is true or not. It was just an old tale. She was just using it to make a point.

"Really, Jotur? I didn't know that," Yves doubts her sincerity. They did almost everything together, and he never remembered doing that.

"So Tredge, the belltower was built to protect us, so if it ever rang, everyone would be able to hear its warning." She pauses and gives Yves a look not to interrupt this time.

"The clang is made to be loud enough to be heard on the village edge, the shoreline, and even out at sea for up to a mile or two for the fishermen. It is to be rung ONLY in times of serious threats."

Yves jumps from the floor, "Like trolls!" he shouts and leaps over to Tredge.

Tredge tries to escape, but it is too late.

"Trolls? I thought they weren't real," Tredge asks as his brother pins him to the floor and begins to tickle him relentlessly.

"Yveesss!" Jotur shouts.

"Yes, huge, ugly creatures that eat children," Yves continues to tickle Tredge as he squirms, laughing and trying to get away. Jotur rolls her eyes at her brothers.

"Okay, okay, I give!" Tredge says to get his brother to ease up.

"No, not trolls! Yves, this could be serious. The bell has only been rung once to warn the Vikings of an approaching army," Jotur says with frustration in her voice, placing her hands sternly on her hips. She is now standing over the boys to get their attention.

"If trolls are real…," Tredge wonders, ignoring his sister and losing interest in the tower. "…wouldn't they attack at night?"

"Of course, they are real," Yves says though he has never actually seen one and isn't sure if he believes in them himself. "Trolls are large, powerful creatures that often raid, plunder, and destroy villages to scrounge for food. They are scary and mean and instinctively follow the light of flickering fires at night to find villages and camps to ravage." Yves can't help himself.

"Now you are just trying to scare me, and I'm not scared!" Tredge crosses his arms across his chest and makes a mean face at his brother.

"Boys!" Jotur shouts, louder than she intends. They halt immediately and look at her, now a target for their outburst.

"She sounds just like mom," Tredge says under his breath to Yves, who nods his head in agreement.

"Yeah, but she's not our mom. We should get her!" Yves whispers back.

Knowing that whispers between her brothers are never good, Jotur turns to run for the door, but the boys are faster than her. They tackle her to the ground.

"Say you give!" Tredge says, tickling her.

"No, say we rule!" Yves teases, encouraging him.

"Yeah, say your brothers rule!" Tredge adds.

"Okay, okay! You rule," she says.

"Who?" Tredge asks, laughing.

"You both...rule...stop...yes, you're both masters of the universe...you are!" Jotur confesses as her sides begin to hurt from laughing so much. She'd say anything to get them to stop, even if she would never hear the end of it. Once she gives in and sits up, she gives Yves the go-ahead to continue his story. Now the three were sitting on the floor, eyes on Yves.

"Okay, as I was saying," Yves continues as they all regain their composure. "Svalbard has never been attacked by trolls, but I have heard tales from the elders and neighboring kinsmen of the horrible things trolls can do. In previous years without a warning system, the trolls left paths of destruction...," Yves pauses, watching Tredge's eyes get bigger and bigger, "and even death," he has to add. "The only survivors were the smallest of

Vikings hidden away by their mothers and only if they didn't make a sound."

"Yves, you know he will believe anything," Jotur says, trying to get him to stop his teasing, but it is useless.

"Not true," Tredge speaks up. "But I do believe in trolls!"

At that moment, as if to reply to the end of his story, the bell rings a second time. *BONGGGG*! It pierces the young Vikings' ears as they attempt to cover them. Jotur looks sharply at Yves, not to say, '*I told you so,*' but in fear. At the second ringing of the bell, Yves is unsure what to believe.

"Are you sure they aren't just ringing them for the festival?" Tredge asks both Yves and Jotur, seeing the expressions on their faces. Without a minute gone by, as if to answer his question, they hear another *BONGGGG!* A third and final toll, the sound seems louder and stronger than the first two, as if taking its final breath.

Jotur turns to Yves, "Go get your weapons." Her brother sits frozen, and she shouts this time, "Yves, get your weapons! One ring could have been an accident, a second a hoax, but three times is definitely not a hoax nor an accident!" she yells. "You need to hide," she tells Tredge. "Take cover!"

"A warning bell, our warning bell, that's all it is," Yves says out loud, talking more to himself than his siblings. '*Maybe, just maybe, it is a test,*' Yves tells himself, and to make sure, he heads to check the front door. As soon as he opens it, he notices a smoldering smell, and when he turns to look toward the village, he knows the bell toll is not a hoax. The small seashore village is under attack. He feels sick to his stomach.

"Oh, no!" he exclaims, "Jotur! Come quick." He stands staring in disbelief. He demandingly motions her to the door. "The village is in trouble." Tredge reaches him first, and Jotur runs up behind him.

"No!" she cries. "Mom and Dad!"

As they all look toward the small village, they can see black smoke circling above it. The three young Vikings watch the smoke twisting miles high and see what seem to be birds flying around in and out of it, descending straight down, then rising above the dark mist again.

"Go get your weapons!" she says. This time Yves listens. "We have to go get Mom and Dad."

Tredge jumps up and runs into the other room, almost bumping into Yves as he returns to the family room with his weapon. After grabbing his father's sword, Yves rushes to the door and looks to the village once again in disbelief. As he steps onto the front porch, he glances over at Tredge by his side, ready to follow his big brother anywhere with his axe in hand. The axe is the only actual weapon Tredge is allowed to carry unless he is out with his father. This situation is no exception, though a spear is his weapon of choice.

"Tredge, it's not safe. You have to stay here," Yves tells him.

"But I want to help," he says, pleading. "I want to help!"

"No, it's not safe," Jotur says firmly as she appears in the doorway with her bow and arrow.

"But I don't want to stay here alone," Tredge says, knowing she won't like the thought of him being at home all alone.

Jotur grabs her father's long sword from Yves' hand and heads to their parents' bedroom. She takes the sword and strikes the lock on an old wooden trunk in the corner of the room, bursting it open. She lifts the top and reaches inside of it, pulling out a coat of chain mail and a small helmet.

"Here, put this on," she hands the two items to Tredge, "…and stay close."

"So, I'm going?" he asks a little too excitedly.

Jotur is scared for her youngest brother to go with them but is more scared of leaving him behind at home. As Tredge slips on the protective chainmail, Yves gets a shield from the trunk and takes back his dad's sword. Now, prepared as much as the three little Vikings could ever be, they head toward the back door to the trail which leads to the village wall. They know a shortcut to the village. Tredge puts on the helmet and holds on to his axe tightly, following close behind his siblings.

The Legends of Trolls and Valkyries

"Okay, stay together," Yves says, taking the lead as they start to step through the bushes leading to a small break in the village wall. He looks at Tredge specifically. Jotur and Yves put Tredge between them as they enter the village.

"We have to find Mom," Yves says, knowing their mother left without a weapon for protection. She never carried one or cared to take up the practice. She always said she had her own personal Viking, their dad, and three little Vikings to take care of her!

"Mom and Dad, you mean," Tredge repeats, making sure they plan to save both of them.

"Yeah, but Mom won't have anything for protection," Yves reminds him, but after he said it, he thought he probably should have kept his worry to himself, especially after seeing the look on his sister's face.

"Well, she has Dad," Tredge says. "That is what she always says."

"Your right, Tredge," Yves says to satisfy him. Yves and Jotur did not know that their parents didn't walk to the village together, and Tredge forgot to mention that detail of the morning's conversation.

"Okay, off to find both of them, let's go," Tredge says like he's leading the way, with no fear whatsoever. His ignorance is bliss; he doesn't know he should be afraid. The closer they get to the wall, the faster they walk, and the closer they get, the harder it is to see or breathe. They can hear only chaos ahead. As they reach the gate to the center of the village, the air thickens with smoke and dust. They each pull cloths up over their noses and mouths and trudge on.

'But it's daylight,' Jotur thinks as she follows Yves and Tredge through the gate. Yves had said that people usually got attacked at night. That is what she had been told, and that is what she has always believed. That is why they always took extra care to lock up the animals,

put the beam over the door for extra security, and why they were usually not allowed out alone when it was dark outside. She pulls Tredge closer and stops immediately on Yves' heels. They were in sight of the marketplace.

As the three young Vikings enter the open courtyard leading to the market area, clouds of dust were beginning to settle just enough to make out shadows. The unusual smells of smoke and debris mix with the scent of fresh flowers gathered from the coastline to be used to adorn the festivities. The oddities of the smells don't compare to the sights. The air, thou fireless at the moment, is still smoldering. The warmth of the lifeless fire has left behind an ascending fuzzy haze. It obscures their vision and burns their eyes.

"This isn't right. Why now? So sudden when we have been safe for so long. Who or what would attack us in the daylight?" Jotur asks out loud, though not expecting an answer. She begins to step into the haze of the courtyard in disbelief.

"Be careful. Watch where you step," Yves tells her as he takes the first step toward the shadows. Slowly the dark shapes come into focus with each step closer. The figures above are still flying down from the sky; following each swoop are screams, human screams.

"Screaming, did you hear that?" Tredge shouts through the cloth covering his face. The once blur of what seemed to be giant birds in the cloud of smoke was not what they had thought at all. They are becoming clearer now, even though the Vikings are peering through a smoky mask. The shapes are becoming more defined with each step closer toward them.

"What are those?" Tredge asks. "Those aren't birds at all!" he exclaims.

"I'm not sure I want to know," Yves says, recognizing the somewhat odd forms from a picture in archives. But, if they are what he thinks they are, he can't believe his eyes.

"That can't be," Yves voices his thoughts. "THEY can't be," he repeats.

But by the look on Yves' face, Tredge knows he remembers something. Tredge looks back at the figures, female figures, and back at Yves.

"Hey, those aren't invaders or birds, aren't they those Val things Dad was telling us about?" he shouts over the chaos around them, bringing Yves thoughts to words.

"Legendary Valkyrie," Yves corrects him in a low dreaded voice. "I can't believe what I am seeing."

"The soul collectors," Tredge confirms. "Cool!"

"Cool?" Jotur interjects. "What is so cool?" she says, beginning to panic. Her heart races with her mind. "The Valkyries are creatures that collect souls of the dead!" she shouts. "Mom!" she cries out. "Dad!"

"Look, they're riding on horses with wings!" Tredge points up to one about to swoop down, not realizing the gravity of the situation.

"What are they doing here?" Jotur grabs Yves and spins him around to look at her. "We've got to find Mom and Dad!" Jotur yells, having a hard time keeping her wits about her.

"Okay, I'll look for Dad," Yves tells her. "Attacks are always swift and merciless, regardless of what they attack. Time is of the essence." He turns as he finishes his sentence and instantly disappears in the smoke heading toward the center of the market. Jotur takes Tredge's hand, pulling him close. The words *'swift and merciless'* linger in her head.

"Be careful, very careful," she tries to tell her brother, but he is already gone. "Follow me, and stay close," Jotur demands, but for once, Tredge doesn't mind. He plans on staying close, very close. They follow their brother into the chaos of smoke, hoping their mother and father will not be far from each other.

The Marketplace

Jotur can see just enough of the destruction through the gloomy mist.

"The marketplace is a wreck," Tredge burst out and points. "Look, that tent is burning." Jotur notices the fire, but before the two of them can take another step, Yves appears with a pail of water and throws it on the burning flames.

"Quick, fetch a pail," he says to Jotur and Tredge, then disappears again. The two look around. Water seems to be scarce, and they have no idea where to look for a bucket. They have no idea how Yves found the one he was using or where he went to fetch water.

"Here," Yves returns with another pail of water and hands a bucket to Tredge. The two work side-by-side to put out one fire while others begin to blaze around them. When they finish putting out the small fire, Yves looks around and realizes this merchant's stock is destroyed. Tredge looks on in defeat.

"I'm sure Mom and Dad weren't anywhere near this place when it went up in flames," Yves tells his brother as he puts his hand on his left shoulder to comfort him.

Jotur, continuing her search, looks across the fragments of the daily market. Its pieces are spread across the town center in shambles. Tables are splintered, chairs broken, canopies ripped into shreds, fabric flung across the cobblestone, and smoke still filling the air.

"It's all in ruins," she shouts to her brothers, still examining the damages of the fire. "Any sign of Mom and Dad?" she asks.

"It seems no place is left untouched," Jotur says as she sits on the ground, putting her head in her hands to hide her tears, the tears she can no longer keep in. "...And the people, the children, where is everyone?" she wonders aloud.

Yves and Tredge walk up and join her, each taking a seat next to her.

"We were too late," Yves says, feeling guilty he didn't take the bell seriously now.

"Was it a troll?" Tredge asks.

"...No, not a troll," Yves says quietly, not wanting to tease anymore. Instead, he just stares into the mist with no expression. He feels frozen with fear, but he doesn't share that. "I never thought...," he trails off, not completing his sentence, still staring into the mist.

"Thought what? Tredge asks.

Jotur is worried more now for their parents, fearing the worst.

"Could it have been trolls?" Jotur asks. Yves has no explanation.

"I thought trolls were just stories," he replies, "or maybe I had always hoped that is the case." The stories spoke of various troll dwellings like caves and isolated rocks far away from the villages. "I thought the stories were so we wouldn't venture out too far or explore the caves."

"But trolls are slow, aren't they?" Tredge asks, always believing.

"Yeah, but they were, or are, deadly creatures that leave destruction in their path," Yves tells him. "As the stories tell, we live far apart from one another, Vikings and trolls, and rarely cross paths…unless the trolls are somehow coaxed out, or worse, unable to find food."

"So they do eat children!" Tredge exclaims.

"No, I was just kidding when I said that…," Yves confesses. "Ah, I don't know."

"…So do they look gruesome too? And how big are they, really?" Tredge asks, full of more questions.

"I've never seen one," Yves tells him honestly. "But I do know one thing; trolls can't be a good sign, especially if they did this!"

Tredge holds the rest of his questions for later. He recognizes his brother and sister are realizing their bedtime stories may have just come to life.

***

Jotur, Tredge, and Yves get up and stand at the market's edge, surveying the damage. They had forgotten about the images flying above since they couldn't see them in the rising smoke. Each one still searches visually for their parents. They scan the area from where they stand, seeing remnants of what used to be a once beautiful landscape with shops and tents filled with flowers, fruits and vegetables, and the freshest fish from the sea. All laid in ruins with the canapé fabrics ripped down and strewn about, vegetables and goods smashed and covering the ground, and the once fresh scent of sea, flowers, and goods slightly linger with the smell of the smoldering smoke. Though some still burn sporadically across the quad, the flames are now beginning to go out on their own. The straw from the rooftops is scattered all over the grounds, and as a result, animals, chickens, rabbits, and pigeons run in circles looking for shelter but can't find any. Jotur, Tredge, and Yves stand scanning the place for a sign of life, any life, but especially their parents. They knew the legends of trolls, but if this was a troll, or worse, more than one, they had never seen destruction like this before today. Minutes seem like hours as they stood motionless, afraid to move. Fearful of what they might find or who.

As the smoke begins to settle, they can see a few Viking men, women, and children figures hidden down on the ground begin to emerge. Only a few survivors hide silently so as not to warn anything or anyone of their presence. Slowly, one by one, they start to surface in search of loved ones. As they stand there, the three Viking children do not say a word in fear of the worst, though they all think the same thing. Not one of them wants to voice their alarming thoughts out loud. *'Where are their parents?'* Tredge grabs Jotur's hand and she squeezes it, holding it as if never to let go. It is Yves who breaks the silence between them.

"Hey, there's Mom and Dad!" Yves exclaims, pointing. Jotur and Tredge look in the direction he indicates, and through the thickness of the smoke, they can just make out an image that looks like their mother. As they approach, they can see it is their mother, only a few yards away, sitting on some fallen straw with Sigvard by her side, consoling her. The thought of their children safely at home comforts them. However, the Viking children aren't very good at staying put, especially when danger is approaching. Tredge begins to run toward them, but Jotur stops him.

"Careful," she says. "There's stuff everywhere. Watch your step," she reminds him.

Tredge begins to shout with excitement over the sight of his parents, but there is no direct path to get to them. Yves looks for a clear passage to no avail.

"Mom, Mom, Dad, OVER HERE!" Yves shouts to get their attention as he tries to approach them. Frightened by the sight of their children, they wave their arms to stop them.

"Stop, Stop!" Sigvard yells, "Go back. It's too dangerous out here!" he shouts. Debris and rubble lie between them. Sigvard is trying to help Elsa to her feet, obviously hurt, and begins to head toward the children to prevent them from running in their direction. Elsa, still waving them back, shouts.

"Stay put; we will come to you," she says, hoping this will protect them from risk. "No! Stay there," Elsa cries again, seeing Yves still trying to move toward them.

She is unable to stand from what looks like an injured ankle.

"We will come to you," their father says, still encouraging them to stay put and out of the view of Valkyries.

As Sigvard and Elsa slowly move toward their children, Sigvard helping Elsa walk, they step carefully to avoid the fallen debris. Neither one notices the Valkyries circling above them, nor do the children. Then, suddenly, Elsa falls, and Sigvard stops to help her back up. Taking this as her queue, one Valkyrie and her gallant horse spiral downward toward them. In an instant, the female figure gracefully lifts Sigvard off the ground. Still holding on to her husband's hand, Elsa is lifted up off her feet and off the ground too.

Jotur realizes what is happening and screams in terror. "Noooooo!" she yells. "They're alive. Stop!" she calls out as if the Valkyrie would listen to a mere mortal.

"Wait," she shouts again. "Come back!" Tredge and Yves watch in fear, frozen from speech.

Elsa holds on tightly as the two rise higher into the smoldering sky. In fear, she glances back at Jotur. Sigvard says to her, "No, honey, don't let go; it's too late." They are up too high now to let go. He tightens his grip and holds on to his wife.

Another Valkyrie flies up underneath them and snatches Elsa away from her husband. They both shout in fear.

"Elsa!" Sigvard shouts, reaching out for her. As Elsa is swept away by the Valkyrie, she turns to look at her children one last time. She watches Jotur, Yves, and

Tredge fade into the cloud of smoke surrounding the village, then loses consciousness.

Standing on the edge of the courtyard, the three young Vikings don't know what to do and are unsure of what they just witnessed.

"They weren't dead, they were waving to us, they were talking to us, they weren't dead!" repeats Yves, still looking up.

"They were still alive," confirms Jotur. "I saw them too, and Mom looked right at me." Tredge looks at Jotur and Yves in confusion and for answers.

"Then why did they take them? They haven't fallen, have they? They were still holding hands, right?" Tredge asks, but Jotur and Yves don't answer him. They had all watched as their parents were flown away into the distance, getting smaller and smaller, fading from their view. They stand there, keeping their eyes on the sky, waiting, hoping for them to be returned. They say nothing, do nothing, frozen in grief.

When they finally do move, Jotur looks around, still in shock. Yves begins to help others who had emerged put out small fires around the quad, taking his mind off what had just happened, speechless. They look under the debris, checking for survivors and hidden children, but no more can be found. Those who did survive are helping the wounded, but few are left. There is no way to tell who was gone.

'*The battle in the village must have been quick,*' Yves thinks. '*Vikings are great warriors,*' he tells himself. '*But trolls are gutless and vengeful. They must have been no match for the trolls, who will kill everyone in their path, even women and children, and can't be reasoned with, like wild animals.'*

Everything had been destroyed. It seemed as if the whole thing was over before the Jorgensen children had ever arrived. Jotur, Yves, and Tredge look around at everything before them in horror. No one speaks of what had just happened. They can't even put it into words.

***

A few days later, the few villagers who survived decide to move away from their now ruined town. Jotur, Yves, and Tredge are left to fend for themselves. Not knowing what else to do, they go back to their chores, working wordlessly. Their regular routine is the best thing for them. It is the only thing holding them together. Though they still have many questions, there is no one left to ask, and they can't put their feelings into words even if they want to. Jotur stays busy with her chores outside to keep the sight of her endless tears from her brothers. She continuously goes over and over what she saw. She can't forget the sight of the Valkyrie flying above the city, the look on her mother's face and in her mother's eyes. The scene is forever sketched into her memory; even if she wanted to forget it, she couldn't. She walks aimlessly outside, thinking to herself. She begins talking aloud, the first time she has heard her voice since the horrific event.

'*The Valkyries are real,*' she says to herself, though only the wind is listening. She had never given it much thought before the raid, but she is beginning to realize the realm of it all. '*If the Valkyries are real,*' she pauses and sits in the middle of the pasture, perched on a rock sticking out of the hillside. She looks up at the sky as if it is going to answer her questions. She comes to a realization, '... *that means Valhalla is real, and then Asgard must be real too. They have to be in Asgard. They took them to Asgard, alive.'* For the first time since that day, she smiles slightly, holding on to just a glimpse of hope. *'But there is no way trolls are real,'* she thinks. *'The village had to be raided by something, but trolls? Seriously?'*

A few days later, at a solemn dinner, she breaks the silence and speaks her thoughts out loud to her brothers. As crazy as it may sound, she has to voice her ideas to them.

"Yves, do you think Valhalla is real?" Jotur trails off in a whispering tone. Both boys stop chewing but don't look up or even attempt to make eye contact with her. The last few days have been as if the three of them were deaf and mute. Grief-stricken by the loss of their parents, they went about their daily routines and chores, not knowing what else to do or how to get by on their own. There is no laughter or playing as there was before, just working wordlessly and seeming aloof to the events that had occurred only a few days earlier. Even Tredge wasn't out in the fields fighting the pigs and cow in an epic battle. Instead, each did whatever mindless duty they could to keep their thoughts of that day far from the forefront of their minds. Each cries silently to sleep at night as if not to awaken the other or admit their pain. Each tries to be stronger for the other. There certainly haven't been any discussions of that day, and the only spoken words were brief.

Jotur, realizing they heard her with their subtle lack of chewing, continues with her thought, "...And if it does exist, do you think it still lies in Asgard?"

She's shocked she had the nerve to bring it up, especially in front of their little brother, but the house has been too quiet, and someone had to break the silence. Yves looks up from his plate. His eyes begin to tear up involuntarily. Seeing Yves' response, she quickly looks down at her picked-over plate of food and tries to brush the thought from her mind regretting ever mentioning it.

"I'm sorry, I'm sorry. I should never have mentioned it," Jotur says, and she stands up to clear the table. She feels she should have kept her thoughts to herself, but she misses sharing them with Yves, her best friend. But now her words were out, and they had already stirred up something in Tredge.

"Why did the Valkyries take our parents?" Tredge asks, still not looking up but beginning to eat again. He was always the last to finish. "They were still alive, I thought," he adds as he pushes a spoonful of beans into his mouth.

Tredge looks as if he has grown up overnight, his spirit crushed from a childhood robbed too early. Jotur hasn't made eye contact with him in days for fear of him seeing right through her tough facade. Afraid he would see she's not the strong and invincible big sister he needs, or see the fear in her eyes, the tears. Afraid he would see how petrified she really is and realize she doesn't know what she is doing. Vikings should be fearless. Now, he asks, *'Why?'* Jotur thought, *'How can Yves and I explain to him something we don't understand ourselves?'* For a long moment, neither of them answers his question. Yves finally speaks up.

"I saw it too; I know I did. They were holding hands," Yves admits out loud for the first time since the incident, "...And I thought the Valkyries only took the dead? Or so I read. The books lied; they're evil," he says angrily, slamming his fist on the table, startling Jotur and Tredge who finally look up. Yves didn't get angry often, but when he did, they knew to leave him alone! But things were different now. There wasn't Mom or Dad to talk to him while the others went out to play. So, Jotur tries to take control of the situation, as her mother often did.

"That's what I have read about them, too," Jotur agrees in a calming voice. "But all the archives are destroyed, aren't they? We can't go back there."

Still staring down at the table, Yves answers, "I read them, I read them all. I know the stories. I know every god, goddess, and all about the mythical creatures...well, I guess they're not so mythical anymore!"

"Do you think there's an exception to the rule?" she asks. If anyone could find a loophole, it would be Yves.

"I don't know," Yves says. He had never thought about it before, but he never had a reason. "Maybe the Valkyries thought they were dead."

"Yeah, like they couldn't hear them calling to each other?" Tredge chimes into the conversation.

Jotur looks over at her youngest brother. *'Tredge, poor Tredge,'* she thinks, finally noticing how badly he needs a bath. *'He's not a baby anymore. We can't shelter him from the world any longer.'*

Yves ignores his questions. He is focused on what Jotur is suggesting. "The Valkyries probably saw the destruction and just figured there were no survivors," he says, trying to rationalize it to himself, then goes back to eating.

This is the most conversation they have had since the incident and enough for the night. The boys finish their meal in silence while Jotur cleans up, all deep in thought. But Yves can't stop thinking about what Jotur said and what he saw. He saw it, too; it wasn't just his imagination. And now that the questions are out there, he wants to know the answers. Now all three of them are thinking about the day they were trying to forget.

The Elder, Ultor

After a sleepless night of tossing, Yves waits until the morning dew thaws off the grounds, grabs his shield, and starts to head toward the village. He's the man of the house now, and it's his responsibility to take care of his brother and sister, though he is just a young boy himself.

"Where we goin?" Tredge asks, jumping off the barrel he sat on, whittling just outside the barn. For a brief second, things seem normal, Tredge wanting to follow Yves wherever he was headed and asking questions along the way. Yves was hoping Tredge and Jotur would be about their morning chores in silence as it had been the last couple of days, so he could quietly sneak off, but that is not the case. Tredge and Jotur have had sleepless nights too.

"You can't go this time," Yves tells him. "You need to stay here with Jotur. It may not be safe."

"I am too going!" Tredge snaps back.

"Where yah going?" Jotur asks as she walks in on the conversation, hearing *'not be safe,'* and *'I am too.'*

"Nowhere, just for a walk," he replies, not looking at her. She can always tell when he is lying.

"Then why can't Tredge go?" she asks, knowing well enough Yves is not just going on a walk. He had his shield and sword with him. "And why isn't it safe?"

"Who are you? My mother?" The words come out of his mouth before he even realizes what he is saying.

Stunned by his reply, she stubs up, and instantly all the tears she was holding in start to fill her eyes. Tredge bows his head, sad at the mere mention of his mother.

"Jotur!" Yves calls out as he steps over to her and puts his arm around her. This is the first time he's shown any compassion or emotions since the incident. "I'm sorry, I didn't mean it like that," he tells her. Though it's something he has said a hundred times before, it didn't sound the same anymore.

Jotur tries to compose herself and looks up at Yves, "So tell me, where are you going?" she asks again.

He can't tell her a lie. He knows he has to tell her the truth.

"I…," he pauses, trying to find the words. He really doesn't want to admit that he is going to the village to look for something. He doesn't want them to know he has lingering doubts about their parents' untimely deaths. He doesn't want to give them false hope by sharing his belief that their parents might still be alive in Asgard.

"…I was just thinking of looking for some of the old archived books, you know, to read."

"No, you want to see if you can find out any more information," Tredge corrects him. "I'm in!" he tells him.

Yves starts to confess. "Yes, information about…," pausing as he looks at Jotur for some kind of expression, a glimpse of what she is thinking, "Asgard," he finishes his sentence. Still, nothing is evident, her face expressionless.

"I know," Yves begins to explain himself to his sister as if he needs to, "I know what I saw, Mom and Dad, they were alive, and they were still talking to us right before the Valkyries took them. I knew it then and didn't want to believe my eyes. We all saw it. It just doesn't make any sense." He realizes how foolish and pitiful it made him seem, holding on to hope that his parents were still alive. Saying it out loud and saying it in his head were two different things.

"Jotur, did you hear me? I'm going to town." Yves now questions if she even heard him at all by her demeanor. "Tredge needs to stay with you, okay?"

But she ignores his last request.

"Wait here!" she responds, running back toward the house and quickly rushing through the door. A few minutes later, she emerges with her bow and boots in hand and an axe. Jotur quickly sits on the porch steps to put on her boots, keeping her sight on Yves to ensure he doesn't sneak off. As she stands back up, pulling on her bootstraps, her foot gently slips into the second boot. She looks up at the boys who are watching her. Yves, agitated with her lack of listening and disappointed he didn't get to sneak off by himself, starts to walk toward her.

"Seriously, Jotur? All of us don't need to go," Yves says as he tries to convince her to stay home one last time. "It won't be a pretty sight," he reminds her to no avail.

"Tredge, come grab your axe!" she yells toward him as she holds it out. "We're going too," Jotur explains.

Tredge jumps in excitement and runs toward Jotur. She is glad to see him smile again, even if only for a second. Once his axe is in hand, he starts to head for Yves, quickly catching up. They start walking toward the village, all three of them now. Tredge starts to pass Yves on the trail to take the lead as he has done many times before, but this time it wasn't a game.

"Wait!" Yves reaches out and pulls on Tredge's arm, stopping him.

"Oww, stop!" Tredge shouts back at him.

"Tredge, listen!" Yves says, not letting go. "It might be dangerous." He looks down at Tredge to make sure he is paying attention. "You can't just lead or run ahead. There might be robbers in the village, and who knows what kind of animals may be lurking around." His voice is stern.

Jotur shrugs at the thought of what they might find and knows Yves is right, albeit a bit abrupt with Tredge. She picks up her pace to catch up to them. "Listen, though what you say may be true, you don't have to be so tough on him."

"I was telling him the truth," Yves snaps. "Like it or not, we are his parents now."

"Maybe so, but you don't have to be so hateful to him," she says. "His loss is no less than yours; his pain is the same."

"Yeah!" Tredge says in agreement.

Jotur turns to Tredge. "Not helping!" She gives a disapproving look. "Now you have to listen to us, no exceptions. Your brother is right. We don't know what we are walking into, and it could be dangerous. Fires could still be burning, making the structures unsafe, or we may find poachers or wild animals. You have to stay close to us, you hear?" she says seriously.

"Us," Yves repeats.

"Now who is being the parent?" Yves says sarcastically. For some reason, when she told Tredge to do something, it just didn't seem as harsh as when Yves said it.

"Boys, it's going to take all three of us, our strength, and standing together if we are to survive. Winter is coming." With that said, Jotur turns to lead the way.

***

Upon entering the gates of the village, the stench of smoldering smoke and ash falls like a thick invisible cloud around them. Jotur takes Tredge by his hand and pulls him closer to her; then, lets go.

"Walk a little closer where I can see you," she whispers.

"Why are you whispering?" he asks. "There's no one here."

"Just in case," Jotur responds, trying to look beyond the mass of ruins where their beautiful market once stood.

"In case of what?" Tredge whispers back.

'Was he not just listening?' Jotur thinks, ignoring the question. It has only been three days since the marketplace was filled with villagers going about their day of trade.

"The entrance doesn't smell like fresh flowers anymore," she notes out loud.

"No, it smells rotten," Tredge replies.

"Now it's all just a skeleton of what it used to be," Yves adds. "Everything is in ruins."

"Yves, where do we start?" Jotur asks, scanning the damage. "I can't tell what's what."

"Closest to the archives, I guess," Yves replies. "So, where would that be?" he asks as he looks around at what's left of the crumbling buildings.

"In case what, Jotur, did you see something?" Tredge asks, still wanting to know why she was whispering in the first place.

"Them, someone, I don't know!" she snaps, not really knowing how to answer his questions at the moment and starting to get annoyed.

"Them who?" Tredge asks. "It's silent," he says, seeing no one and hearing no one.

"Starting back to your old ways of asking questions, I see," Yves says, feeling a bit of comfort in the normalcy of his constant questioning. He is actually a bit relieved to hear his brother speak after his silence the past few days. Yves reflects on how he used to think he would bless the day when his brother would run out of questions to ask. But Tredge's pestering never seemed to bother him as much as it did Jotur; he could always just ignore him.

"I don't know, Tredge! Stop with the questions; I'm trying to think." Jotur says in a sharper tone.

Jotur scans the scene and shrugs her shoulders, "I guess we can start on the left of the quad and move to the right, but together, don't spread out. We don't know what could be hiding under all this debris."

"Aaghhh, like what? That was my question in the first place!" Tredge asks.

"Well, we are about to find out," Yves says, taking the first step toward the rubble.

"Tredge, be careful and stay close. Even though this stuff isn't burning, its structure is weak, and any of it could shift at a moment's notice."

"You already said that, sis!" Tredge reminds her. He doesn't know whether to be thankful they are treating him more like a peer or if he would prefer to revert back to his joyful childhood. He would have done anything just a few days ago to get his big brother's attention and have him treat him this respectfully, but now he would take it all back just to see his parents again.

After an hour of searching through broken down wood and debris, carefully lifting piece by piece looking for some resemblance of town records, Jotur says, "Anything boys? A book? A Record? Papers?" she asks despairingly.

"A Survivor?" Yves replies in amazement as he lifts a large piece of wood that lay just over what use to be a trade shelter.

"Very funny," she says, not thinking his joke was in good taste.

"No, seriously, a survivor!" He says again, this time very seriously.

Jotur and Tredge run over to where Yves is standing, having stretched the distance between their 'sticking together' rule of thumb over the last hour. They saw nothing but a pile of rubble. Both just stare down at the area in which Yves is looking. He bends down, lifts a board off the stack, and throws it to the side.

"Wait, be careful!" Jotur says, putting her hands up as if to stop Yves. "We don't want anything else to collapse on him...or her, if someone is buried underneath all this." His sister looks at him as if to tell him something he doesn't know. *'It could even be a child,'* she thinks, eyeing her brother. Yves, realizing what she is trying to tell him, takes the cue and looks at Tredge.

"Tredge, could you get us something to pry up the other boards?" Yves sends him on an errand just in case. They don't know what they are digging up, and if they can shelter Tredge from any more tragedy, they will.

"Do you think they're alive?" Jotur whispers to Yves out of earshot of Tredge, some hope in her voice.

"I heard something. It sounded like words." He looks at his sister, glad they are communicating again.

"Seriously?" She freezes, stopping all movement to listen for a sound. A sign of life. She moves her head closer to the rubble. "I don't hear anything."

Yves follows her lead and puts his head down close to the rubble, trying not to draw Tredge's attention. Just as he does so, the pile of rubble speaks, giving out a weak but still sharp, "Go away!"

"Did you hear that?" Yves asks, hearing the small whispering sound again emerge from below.

"Yeah, sounds like, 'GO AWAY!'," Tredge says. They had their ears so close to the ground concentrating they didn't see Tredge was back and watching them.

"No, it was 'CLEAR AWAY!'," Jotur clarifies.

Yves and Jotur begin to dig frantically, forgetting to be so careful with the excitement of a survivor, delighted to no longer be alone in the ghostly village. Tredge watches intensely. Yves finds the first hand.

"Here, over here!" he shouts.

They soon have the whole arm, and then the body to which it is connected, thank goodness, and they pull an old man out of the debris. It is Ultor, the eldest man in the village. He is an old Viking with a long white beard, braids down the front, and extremely large ears.

"Here, give him some water," Jotur says as she hands Yves a small leather satchel filled with water. Yves carefully lifts the water to the old man's mouth and the elder Ultor takes a sip slowly, then tries to speak, but his mouth is dry from the days without water.

"Itsh gogwas gothway," he tries to speak, then takes another sip.

"It was '*go away*,'" he says quietly.

"Ha, I was right!" Tredge says, looking at the other two rather proud of himself.

Ultor is called by the village children *the elephant elder* though he doesn't seem to mind the attention. He has fought in famous battles in his time, but on the day of the trolls' attack, he was too slow to escape the falling building and too old and feeble to battle or defend the village even if he had managed to get into the fight.

"What do you mean?" Jotur asks, "You want us to leave you? You don't want us to save you?" she asks, confused that he is ungrateful for their rescue.

"Did you think we were robbers?" Tredge asks, thinking that makes more sense.

"Yeah, did you think we were just some robbers, and you wanted us to leave?" Yves asks again, agreeing with Tredge's analogy. Stunned by Ultor's reaction to a rescue, Yves helps him to sit up and hopes he can explain his reaction. While they are happy to find another Viking, it seems odd that Ultor is so ungrateful.

"I knew exactly who you were from the very moment you walked into this shambles of a village. I watched your parents grow up, all three of you grow up to what you are now, and fought alongside your grandparents." Ultor stresses by no means is he hiding from robbers and a coward or that he is old and doesn't know what he is saying.

"Then why did you tell us to leave you alone?" Tredge only voices what they are all wondering.

"I want to die in battle," Ultor clarifies. "I want to die defending my village." He sees the look on the kids' faces full of confusion, so he explains further.

"I just want one more fight for the opportunity to earn great honor, to receive the greatest reward, Asgard. Only the greatest of warriors are allowed into Asgard." Finding his voice, finally, he begins ranting about Valkyries, Valhalla, Asgard, and Odin, shaking his fist at the sky, then looking down at the ground and kicking the dirt. The children don't know what to think and can only make out a few words between his grumbling.

"Curse old age," he says. "If I could have gotten out and fought, I would be in Valhalla today!" he shouts to either the sky or the children; they don't know which, but he is definitely mad at someone.

"Now, I will never see Valhalla," he continues. "Instead, I will die of old age and end up in Nifilhel with the others who didn't die in the glory of battle." Ultor had been a great warrior and had even killed a troll before, as told in the village archives, but only warriors who die in battle are chosen to go to Valhalla, no matter how greatly they have fought throughout their lives.

The children just watch as Ultor explains his actions. Once Ultor has calmed down, he starts to account the minutes that led up to him being trapped by the collapse of the building. "It was sudden," he says. "The trolls' attack had been swift at the Thor Tower. No one had any warning. One moment you hear the rustling of hooves, the chatter of men and women, the laughter of children, and the next, total chaos. Everyone was excited about the festival; no one saw it coming, no one!" he repeats to himself as the horrors of the sink in.

"The children were all playing out in the open, no warning…and the bells, who had time to ring the bells?" He looks at the once powerful tower, which now stands half burnt and black from smoke. "They were rung only after the attack had begun," he speaks softly, remembering it was the first time he had heard them in a very long time. "They were already within the village, the trolls, they were destroying everything, people were scrambling to get to shelter, no one was prepared to fight, no one." He plops down onto the ground bowing his head. The children help him sit on a clear spot of cobblestone covered with dirt, spellbound and hanging on his every word. He continues, "Most of the villagers had been unarmed and fought with anything they could find, pitchforks, rakes, rocks, even food, but the trolls' ambush was fierce and merciless, and the whole brawl lasted only minutes." Upon hearing Ultor's account of the horrifying event, the three young Vikings stood silently, not knowing what to say.

Ultor took their silence as an invitation to continue. "I saw the Valkyries coming as the trolls departed," Ultor pauses, reaching for the water bag, "but the damaged building gave way before I could escape and trapped me. I thought your parents had survived, but I guess they were taken too." He takes a drink, avoiding eye contact with the now orphaned Jurgenson children, ashamed he could not have saved their parents or anyone else; he was a very proud man.

Tredge has a thought that never crosses the minds of Jotur and Yves. He utters simply as if the answer was obvious, "If those Valkyries could come and take our parents, and they are real, why can't we go get them back?" he asks. Silence falls among them all. The children turn to their elder for answers, but Ultor has no response to this question. He thinks it is rhetorical, but he sees the young Vikings are waiting for an honest answer. He doesn't know where to start to explain the rules of the gods, but in Yves' and Jotur's minds, they think Tredge's innocent and simple views could sometimes be a gift.

Yves finally breaks the silence by saying, "That's crazy, we...."

He is immediately interrupted by Ultor, who says, "That's impossible."

"Why?" Tredge asks, putting his fist on his hips, offended his ideas are never accepted or taken seriously.

"I don't know. It just is impossible," Ultor says again.

"Has anyone tried to look for Bifrost?" Jotur asks the elder, now beginning to wonder herself.

"Don't know if anyone has ever given it much thought," Ultor answers. A few days ago, he would have been mortified at such a discussion. He doesn't think it is forbidden, but maybe it was; no one ever considered looking for Bifrost or questioning the gods.

"But if no one has ever tried it before, then it's not necessarily impossible, right?" Tredge asks. His logic makes sense to Jotur and Yves, but they are young and naive too.

"Possible or impossible, it makes no difference. Asgard would be a long journey for such young Vikings, and even if you did find it, you can't question the gods."

Yves speaks up, ignoring Ultor's last statement. "It might just work," he says, shocking Jotur and Tredge. "We have nothing else to lose." The siblings exchange looks. He was right; what did they have to lose?

"Well, I don't want to stay here all winter just surviving," Jotur says as she begins to get to her feet, tired of sitting in the ruins of her once beautiful childhood city. That's what it will always stay now, just a memory of her childhood. She reflects as she stands and looks around, watching the last of the floating ashes still falling from the sky downward like a feather to the ground. The city would be forever remembered as it was either before or after the attack. It would never return to its glory days; no one was here to repair or rebuild it. It wouldn't be recreated, she realizes. No one was left living in the town; any skilled carpenters, smiths, or artisans who survived the attack had moved out of the city walls to the hills for the winter. Svalbard was abandoned and demolished, and an elder and three young Vikings couldn't put it back together.

"What do we have to lose?" she says, realizing their situation.

"Your lives," Ultor says, knowing they needed hope for some kind of future, but what was he to do, lie to them?

"It could work," Tredge says, feeling empowered. The three have been in limbo for the last few days with no direction. They were finally talking again and finally seeing a plan for the future. It made them feel enabled.

"Wait, have you three not been listening? Was I not clear? You can't find Asgard, you can't make the journey, and you can't question the gods," Ultor says, upset they aren't listening to him. He is used to being the all-wise Viking in the village, respected for his age and wisdom. He is not used to being questioned. The children don't mean to be disrespectful, but things are different now. From the looks of it, they are all that is left of their beloved city. The three Vikings turn and look at Ultor.

"What?" he asks as the three just look at him. "I told you, it's crazy."

"Do you want to go with us?" Tredge asks innocently.

"We will need a guide," Jotur says.

"…and we need a fighter. You know everything, and you're brave," Yves says, knowing that mentioning bravery and fighting might convince him. Yves also knows their chances of survival are increased significantly with Ultor accompanying them.

Ultor smirks just a bit at the 'you know everything' remark and lifts his chin. "Yes, well, I have traveled quite a lot and know my way around a sword as well as the seas; I am a Viking, you know." He realizes that getting the kids out of the town to a milder winter, or maybe a sister camp where they would be safer, could be a possibility. If they need to dream of finding their parents on the journey, then so be it. They can dream of Asgard.

"Okay, okay, I'm in," Ultor says. "But let's remember who the elder is here."

The three nod their heads in agreement.

"Yeah, we are going on a journey!" Tredge says, feeling relieved there is an adult back in charge, *'Even if he is a hundred years old,'* or so he thinks. Jotur isn't as relieved. She is unsure if Ultor will survive such a journey, but he can't stay and survive alone through the winter, either. Plus, they were family. All Svalbard Vikings are family, and you don't leave family behind. The children help Ultor to his feet and begin walking home, three plus one now. For the first time in days, they are talking, and smiles can be seen once in a while. They are excited for their journey to begin.

"We know that the great rainbow bridge Bifrost connects us to Asgard. So, how can we find Bifrost?" asks Jotur.

"I have seen it, haven't you?" Tredge asks honestly.

"Have we not all seen it?" asks Ultor sarcastically. "I have seen the lights flash from its surface far off in the northern sky many times before."

"We know it lies to the north," says Yves, "but how do we find it? No one knows where it lies."

"Then we must venture north to seek Bifrost," says Jotur, "or at least to find someone who may know its location. We will sail on the Northern Sea in our parents' boat and find Bifrost."

"Hey, if we could reach Bifrost and get into Asgard, maybe I could remain there or in Valhalla, and your parents could return with you." Ultor hates giving them false hopes, but maybe, they will find another village on their journey, and his last Viking duty would be to find a home for the children. Right now, the thought of Bifrost gives them hope, and that is what they need to survive. The remainder of the day is spent gathering provisions, which are somewhat scarce since most have been taken by the trolls or smashed and destroyed. They do, however, have whatever is in their own garden and pantry. The plan is to set sail at dawn.

***

That night Yves can't sleep. He walks into the kitchen and finds his sister looking out the window.

"You can't sleep either?" he asks.

"Do you really think we can find Bifrost?" she asks, hiding the tears in her eyes.

She remembers the last dinner they all had as a family in that very room. Sigvard was making funny faces at the kids as they were trying not to spit out their food when they laughed.

Elsa, trying not to encourage him, had said, "Honey, they are going to choke on their food if you don't stop it," though she couldn't help hiding her own amusement.

"Besides," her mom asked him, "What good is a talent like that? You'll be cast out of the village with a face like that!"

"To scare the children," Tredge answered.

Then her mother made a funny face back at them, and they all laughed. That was the last night the whole family was together.

CHAPTER II

SEARCHING FOR BIFROST

. . . .

Preparing for a Long Voyage

Ultor stays on the boat that night to ready everything to leave the next morning. He also thinks it's not a bad idea for him to keep a watchful eye. The children had loaded the boat with food and equipment as soon as they returned from the village with Ultor. None of them wanted to stay another night in their empty home as a reminder of their parents' absence. Still, Ultor encouraged them to get a good night's sleep and that it would be best to leave at daybreak. The boat was loaded with all they had to survive the winter, journey or no journey. With a ship full of goods, Ultor didn't want anyone to get any ideas, even though he hadn't seen a single person since he emerged from the rubble but the children. The village was empty, and the shore seemed deserted. However, wild animals still roamed the area, and he wasn't taking any chances with their provisions.

At dawn, when the cock crowed, the children gathered their things, fed the animals one last time, and released them out in the fields.

"Do you think they'll be okay?" Jotur asks, hoping her horse will be alright.

"Of course, they're animals," Yves answers. "They've survived all this time before us."

"Well, I just hope whatever destroyed the village doesn't come for them," she replies.

"Don't worry. They are free to roam," he reassures her. "Though they usually don't go far from home anyway, they should be fine," Yves reassures her again as he unlatches the gate and props it open with a rock. Although, he wonders himself if they will be okay.

"Now you stay safe, take shelter, and keep away from the wild animals!" Jotur tells her horse as if he understands. She had had him since she was a young girl, and being so tame, he just stands there looking at her.

"Come on," Jotur tells him. "You're free...go!" she nudges him a bit to get him to pass through the gate. As she does, he gives out a big neigh as if he is talking back. Yves laughs aloud.

"He's telling you not to be so pushy," Yves jokes.

"Very funny." Jotur gives her brother a smirk, though she is glad to see he is back to teasing a little. All three young Vikings seem to have a renewed sense of hope after finding Ultor. And the idea of a new adventure ahead has given them a focus.

"Neeeeeha," he neighs again as he begins to run into the open field with the other animals. They all seem happy to be out in the brisk morning sun, not understanding they are now going to be entirely on their own.

Yves walks off to finish his chores, with Tredge coming out of the house and quickly catching up with him. Immediately the questions begin for the day.

"So, let me get this straight," Tredge has to ask. "You are doing your chores, but we are leaving the farm?"

Yves doesn't answer quickly enough.

"Why? We don't know when we will be back." Tredge looks up at his brother for the answers.

"Well, obviously, we need to free the animals, so they have a better chance to survive, and giving them one last meal before we leave would be nice too, wouldn't it?"

Yves responds as he shovels the last of the hay from the barn into the pasture. "Survive? You mean there's a chance the animals won't survive? Mr. Swiney may not make it?" he asks, looking at his brother now with a concerned look, almost angry for him to even suggest such a thing. Mr. Swiney is not only his favorite pig but the first pig he actually saw come into this world. He helped his mother and sister in delivery, and from that day forward, he took full responsibility for him. Not to mention the numerous battles they had undertaken together. It's not like they didn't have a dozen other pigs around the farm or that they hadn't delivered five more pigs that same day. But Mr. Swiney was the littlest piglet in the litter, and Tredge took an immediate shining to him. He became more of a pet than a farm animal. His mom had to make him start leaving the pig outside at night and out of his bed when he got too big, but Tredge would sneak him back into the house when everyone was asleep.

"Can we take him with us?" Tredge has to ask.

"Who?" Yves is more focused on his own thoughts than Tredge's wondering questions.

"Mr. Swiney, can we take him with us?" he asks again.

"Sure, if we get hungry, we will have some fresh food!" Yves jokes, knowing eating Mr. Swiney is a sore subject.

"NOOO!" Tredge shouts.

Yves laughs, "Well, I don't think we have room for a pig in the boat anyway."

"Good, I think he should stay here too," Tredge now agrees with the plan to leave the animals. He helps gather the last of the feed to give his pig a final meal, wraps his arms around Mr. Swiney's big belly, and says a tearful goodbye. Jotur walks over to the boys, warmed by Tredge's goodbye scene.

"Are you done?" she asks Yves.

"Just now, what do you need?" he asks. He places the pitchfork against the barn wall as he had done every day for the last five years and turns toward Jotur.

"Nothing, I just got the house closed up for winter." She wonders if there is anything else that needs to be done. "The shutters are closed, storage is locked up. Is there anything else we need to do?" she asks Yves, who shrugs.

"No, not that I can think of. We can only do our best to leave it protected, but if someone really wants to get in there, they'll get in," Yves tells her, knowing the risks of leaving an empty house.

"Don't tell me that! I don't want to think about someone else in our house using our stuff," she responds.

"Okay, it is safe then," he tells her. "There is nothing to worry about it." He lies to make his sister feel better, but once they leave the farm, there is nothing they can do about it.

"Tredge, do you have everything?" Yves asks.

"Already at the boat," he responds. Tredge had everything loaded the night before in anticipation.

With the animals fed and freed, supplies loaded, and the house locked up, the three little Vikings are ready to embark on their journey.

"Okay, so let's go!" Tredge tells his siblings and takes the lead to walk to the boat. Each one turns back to take a last look at the farm, the only home they have ever known, but they continue to head down to the shore, where Ultor sits watching and waiting patiently.

"Ultor seems as if he has made peace with being alive," Yves says, observing the old Viking, who looks as if he is prepared for battle, not sailing. Perhaps having a new adventure before him, or another chance to die honorably and earn his rightful place in Valhalla, or possibly just the feeling of being useful again, has rejuvenated him. Either way, Yves is glad to have him along.

Jotur, walking toward the shoreline, looks over her shoulder and takes a deep breath.

"Are you okay?" Yves asks.

"It's surreal," she admits. "Who knew?"

"I know," Yves replies. "Everything is different now."

"Who knew what?" Tredge jumps into the conversation from steps ahead of them. He never seems to be paying attention but always manages to hear everything.

"Nothing," she says, wanting to be alone in her thoughts.

"Well, maybe I know." Tredge can never let things just go. They roll their eyes at the youngest brother and continue walking. Yves lets Tredge get farther ahead before he speaks again.

"Seriously, are you okay?" Yves asks quietly again. They both watch Tredge walk ahead clumsily, stumbling over the rocks, axe in hand.

"Look, he can't wait to show Ultor his axe," she responds, ignoring his question and watching Tredge lovingly. She does not look up at Yves for fear of making eye contact with him. She can see Tredge showing off his axe to Ultor. It was painted with gold and green paint, done by Tredge and his father, and adorned with the emblem of Svalbard. He was very proud of it.

"It's hard," she speaks up after they watch Tredge enter the boat safely. Yves can see the tears in the corner of Jotur's eyes as she speaks. "This is all we have ever known." She takes another deep breath through her nose and smells the brisk morning sea air.

"Do you think we will ever see it again?" she asks her brother. This is the first time in generations their family's homestead would be left abandoned. "Are we doing the right thing?" she wonders out loud.

"Of course," he answers. "We'll be back before you know it." Yves says this so reassuringly he almost convinces himself. He knows quite well the home will be overrun by the hillside in a matter of months; the livestock will have to leave to look for food if they don't return soon, and the harsh climate of the north will take a toll on the empty shack, but he keeps all these thoughts to himself.

"It will be fine," he tells her and gives her a sideways hug. They both know he doesn't know for sure if they will be okay, but they know they aren't okay here, not right now.

Yves begins to walk off to give his sister some time to compose herself before she joins them. He calls ahead to Tredge, now on the boat and asking Ultor questions. He looks back at his sister as he reaches the shoreline. She mouths, "Thank you," to Yves without a sound. He knows they need to be strong for Tredge, who doesn't understand the gravity of the situation, and she needs a moment to gather herself. Jotur takes one last mental picture of her childhood home and turns to walk. This time she doesn't look back again but focuses on watching Yves climb into the boat. She knew Yves was just trying to make her feel better when he said everything would be fine, and she appreciates it. She knows very well that she may never see her home again. *'But it isn't home anymore,'* she tells herself, *'not without Mom and Dad.'*

"Are you ready?" Yves hollers to Ultor as he enters the boat. He can see that Ultor has been making preparations for the trip. The elder stands at the base of the lower mast in his chain mail, shod with steel boots, crested with a winged helmet, and armed with an axe and a sword. He looks much younger and fiercer, ready for a full-on battle.

"Wow, that's amazing stuff," Yves remarks. Ultor definitely has Tredge's attention, who is sitting right next to him, touching everything.

"Where did you get all that stuff?" Tredge picks up Ultor's sword. "Stand your ground!" Tredge shouts, trying to lift the sword parallel to the ground.

Ultor laughs, "It's quite heavy for such a young boy."

"I'm not so young," Tredge reminds him. "Take that, you fire-breathing dragon!" Tredge tries to lunge at the imagined dragon with the heavy sword.

Jotur, composed now, walks up to enter the boat and sees Ultor laughing, which is a first. *'Perhaps he needs us as much as we need him,'* she thinks to herself. She glimpses over at Tredge's fight.

"Taking down a mighty dragon, I see," she says, encouraging him. He is still a boy, so young and impressionable. After so much loss these past few days, it is good to see him play again. She is glad to see that gleam of excitement and life back in his eyes.

"I have a feeling Tredge has a new favorite," she whispers to Yves.

"That's okay. I think I can handle a break," he admits.

"Ultor, have you ever fought a dragon?" Tredge asks, still attacking the air with a massive smile on his face. "Where else have you gone? Where's the farthest place you have traveled to?" Tredge begins to ask questions as fast as his mind can think of them, not allowing time for Ultor to answer.

"There will be plenty of time for Ultor to tell you all about...," Jotur is cut off as Tredge interrupts with excitement.

"The one about the troll you killed right through the eyeball?!" Tredge pleads as he takes the sword and pretends to stab the troll. "Does a troll have a heart? Does he bleed purple?" he asks. "What if he survived? He would be a one-eyed troll!"

"What?" Ultor wonders where Tredge gets his ideas. "We have to get going, but I will tell you what stories I can in time," Ultor says, taking his sword carefully from the dragon slayer and patting Tredge on the head. Ultor did like the attention, though. It had been so long since he had any company, but Tredge had more energy than he could muster up.

"Tredge, right now we need focus," Jotur says, trying to get his attention onto something more productive.

"Yes," Yves says, trying to help with the redirecting. "There will be plenty of time for stories later. We have a long way to go." Tredge takes his seat right next to Ultor. Though quieted by his brother and sister, he watches Ultor closely.

None of them know exactly how far they have to go or if it is even possible to find Bifrost, but at least it has taken the sadness out of their eyes and lightened their hearts to have a glimpse of hope of finding their parents. Yves and Tredge begin to raise the sails as they have done many times on fishing trips with their father. He always said they are excellent sailors. Soon the faithful winds of the Northern Sea fill the sails, and they are off. The winds move the boat steadily from the shoreline, and all watch as the farm and dock fade into the dense fog. The sun has barely breached the horizon, and the mist is heavy on both land and sea as they depart. The boat quiets as each is deep in their own thoughts. The unfamiliar has Yves and Jotur longing to turn around. However, Ultor appears stronger than ever and is eager to renew his taste for adventure.

***

Several days pass as the boat moves slowly northward and somewhat west. There is nothing to break the solitude of their confinement on the small vessel but the ever more frequent icebergs. As the days wear on, the fog lifts, contributing to visibility, but the sky remains overcast and dark. Winter is drawing near, harvest is passing, and the sea air is becoming bitterly cold. The mist settles dew on their faces making it seem even colder. Even Tredge is quiet now with his questions and spends most of his time whittling.

At night the children gather around Ultor's knees and listen to his stories. It has been a while since anyone has shown interest in his old stories, but now he has little ears hanging on his every word. It has already become a habit for Tredge at bedtime. At first, he thought his stories would be a good distraction from the long journey and take the children's focus off their loss. He worries about if he can find them a new home, a place where all three could be together and where he knows they would be safe. He has made this his personal mission, his last deed, knowing it is unlikely they will actually see their parents again. He has never heard of anyone making it to the Bridge of Bifrost, let alone Asgard. His goal is to find them a home.

One night, as Tredge is getting ready to hear the next saga of Ultor's latest quest against the mighty dragon, he takes a seat on a pallet made of hay and blankets, looks up at Ultor, and asks, "How old are you?"

"Old enough to know the trees, the wind upon our bow, and to know what is best for you," he points to Tredge, just barely touching his nose.

Jotur looks over and smiles. She is comforted by not being the oldest one, although she feels old and tired from the weight of the past few weeks, and yet, at the same time, she feels childlike, afraid, and scared of the future ahead.

"That's not an answer," Tredge rebukes as he adjusts the straw underneath his head to prop it up. After ten minutes of rooting, he is finally comfortable and ready to listen.

"Well, let's see, where did I leave off last night? Or, should I say, where did you fall asleep?" Ultor chuckles as he looks to the sky to see the stars, but the fog is so thick he can barely see the end of the boat.

"I think we left off last night when I was about to enter the Norse Mill Cave. The only way is by sea...," Ultor stops. He feels a slight jerk in the forward motion of the boat.

"What was that?" Ultor asks.

"Nothing," Tredge responds, not wanting Ultor to be interrupted from his storytelling.

"No, there was something," Ultor says, looking toward the prow where Yves sits, keeping watch.

"I don't know; it's so dense tonight I can't see anything," Yves answers. "I don't think it's an iceberg." The noise, ever so lightly, comes again.

"Hey, listen!" Jotur waves her hand at them, motioning them to stop talking. Tredge sits up to listen.

"Don't you hear something?" she asks, noticing a sound off in the distance. The boat falls silent as they listen. The sail flips lightly in the breeze. Yves can hear the water slightly splash from the rough surface of the sea as it hits the side of the boat. He listens closer, eliminating the sounds he knows.

"Yeah, I hear it too," Yves whispers after a few minutes. "It sounds more like the waves are breaking gently on something."

"I hear nothing," Ultor says. "You two are just tricking yourselves into believing you hear things. We've been at sea so long you are hearing things." But Ultor's' hearing isn't the best at his age.

"Yes, like waves on a surface," Jotur concurs. The two glance at one another with excitement. They both can't wait to step foot on dry land again.

"Are we there?" asks Tredge, looking at the smiles on Jotur's and Yves' faces.

"Yeah, we are just looking for a dock to park the boat," Yves says sarcastically, and they all chuckle.

Abruptly an earsplitting noise screeches, and they all four jump up. It is followed by a moan or aching sound coming from the boat, the bottom of the boat. This time the noise is much closer, right underneath them.

"Have we run into a monster?" Tredge asks. "Did you hear that, Ultor?" Tredge asks, grabbing Ultor's hand. "It sounds like a monster is under us!"

"Actually, it's probably just the boat scrapping the bottom," Ultor reassures him.

"The bottom of the sea?" Tredge exclaims. He wonders how the boat could touch the bottom of the sea.

"Not the BOTTOM of the sea, Tredge. We have reached a shoreline of some kind." Jotur knows how he thinks. Very literally.

"The shore?" Yves asks, not believing her. He's confused about how they could be at the shore already. He is unsure of their location.

"Isn't it too soon?" Yves turns to Ultor and asks his expert opinion.

"I don't know. It is too dark to tell," he answers and reaches back for a lantern. "We are probably just in shallower waters," Ultor tells them to put them at ease. He doesn't know where they are either and won't until he can see daylight but hopes his answer will satisfy them. It doesn't.

"I can't see anything," says Yves.

"Me neither," Tredge agrees, leaning his head out as far out as he can. All four Vikings are now standing at the front of the boat, looking forward, seeing nothing.

"Let's see if another torch will help," Yves suggest as he grabs the nearest torch and lights it. He stretches as far as he can reach without falling in. "I still can't see anything," he confesses. Regardless they can't get a glance of what lies ahead of them. The fog is so thick it is as if they are in a cloud. All they can see is the reflection of the fire in the mist, making a soft glow and shining no light upon the water or assumed shoreline. Ultor grabs one of the Vikings' fishing poles, leans over the stern, and casts it into the cold water, hitting sand about four feet down.

"Yep, shallow waters," he confirms his suspicion. The boat floats slowly as the four feet become three and then stops. It is now lying just a few feet from dry land.

"Hey, I know that sound," Tredge says, recognizing the unique sound of small waves meeting the shore.

"Yep, we hit ground," Ultor says with excitement.

"The tide must be stronger than we predicted," Yves says. "The tide is on our side!"

"Well, that's encouraging!" Tredge says.

"Maybe it's a good sign," Jotur says, trying to stay positive, knowing they must now leave the safety of the ship to which she has become accustomed.

"Well, either way, we aren't going any father today," Ultor tells them. "Let's get some shuteye while we can." They all take his cue and begin to lay down for the evening. Tredge, excited about the possibility of hitting land, forgets about Ultor's story and instead starts dreaming of what lay just a few feet away from him on dry land.

***

The Vikings stay on the boat through the night until they can see where they are. It is early morning when the haze lifts enough to see where the vast winds have pushed their little ship. When they can finally see more than two feet in front of them, they notice they are in a bay. They are surrounded by land on three sides with an outlet just a mile wide behind them. Astonished at the site, the four of them survey the landscape and realize that, with the force of the tide, they have come to rest on the west side of the inlet.

"So, if we can't row against the wind, then what do we do?" Yves asks Ultor. Now he isn't so sure about the tide being on their side.

"Gees, we are lucky. We could have missed the bay opening and ended up on the rocky shoreline," Tredge exclaims, putting it all into perspective.

"Yes, thanks, Tredge. We are so blessed to be stuck in this icy cove with no way out for our boat." Sarcasm came easy for Jotur, especially this early in the morning. Ultor informs them that they are probably on the large island of Greenland, a land that has always been covered in ice, and that they had drifted northwest when they really needed to sail northeast to avoid the land.

Ultor continues, "I have journeyed over much of this land and to its northern coast." He is concerned they may be drifting too far away from the bordering Viking villages and is hoping to redirect the children. "We must still travel far if we are to reach Bifrost, and we will still need a boat on the northern coast of this land." They have reached their first obstacle and have to decide how to proceed. The Vikings carefully pack up their food and shelter in order to carry it with them, all while discussing a plan.

"We could drag the boat over the land. It is all covered with ice, and the boat could glide easily," Yves suggests. Unfortunately, the boat is much too heavy for them to push or pull and they cannot move it onto the shore, much less move it across the land.

"It's better to make the right decision than to act in haste and have to backtrack," Ultor advises. "We need to be sure of the direction we want to go before we proceed."

The day is growing old, and they haven't moved anywhere.

"Let's rest here again tonight, warm up by a fire, and eat something to gather our strength. We can decide which direction to take and leave early in the morning," Yves suggests.

"Yeah, I need the rest…off the boat." Jotur agrees.

"Awe, man, I wanted to go…somewhere!" Tredge voices his disappointment.

"I agree. An early start is best," Ultor responds with the final word. *'Yves is right,'* he thinks. They will need the daylight to travel on land. Land harbors more dangerous creatures, tribes, and natural disasters ready to happen. He needs to keep these children safe; it is his mission. Tredge begins to set up camp by gathering some wood and helping Yves start a fire. The sky is starting to become clearer, which means it will get very cold. Jotur unpacks some food and begins to heat it upon the fire as the boys prepare the camp.

"Hopefully, things will be clearer in the morning, literally," Yves says as he fixes a pallet to sleep on next to his sister.

As they settle down to eat, Tredge remembers Ultor's story. "What about the dragon?" he asks.

Ultor, unable to resist the opportunity to tell his stories, starts where he left off, at the Norse Mill Cave, and soon Tredge is fast asleep. They all hope morning will bring a resolution to their problem on how to proceed through Greenland. As Yves lays his head down to try to sleep, he looks to the sky. He can once again see the rainbow bridge of Bifrost in the sky. This is the first time he has been able to see it since they left on their journey. It doesn't seem any closer.

The Greenlanders

The next morning, Jotur raises her head, stretches, and slightly opens her eyes to the sight of surprise.

"Look!" Jotur whispers, poking Yves, amazed at the sight before her eyes. He is sound asleep. She leans over to Yves and slowly whispers again in his ear. "Yves, wake up Tredge. He's got to see this!"

Yves rolls over, with his eyes still closed, and not so gently nudges his brother, who had snuck over to them in the middle of the night. "Get up! Jotur wants something," he says in a mumble.

"Yeah, what?" Tredge gets out. He also isn't a bright-eyed morning person, at least for the first five minutes of his awakening. It takes him a few minutes, but once he is awake, the questions continue until he's out again.

"Shush, just look!" Jotur says, loud enough for them both to hear but still in a whisper. They look at her, scared something is wrong. Not wanting to make any sudden movements, she points with her eyes off to the right. The boys gently turn to see what her fuss is about and notice they are surrounded by reindeer. The reindeer, silvery gray in color, match the various stones that line the shore, and when motionless, they seem to fade into the scenery, presence unbeknown.

"Wow!" Tredge whispers.

"Where's Ultor?" Yves asks.

Jotur shrugs her shoulders. "I just woke up and found them surrounding us," she confesses.

"That's a good sign," a voice says to the children. "The reindeer like you." At that moment, Ultor appears. He walks up, not at all worried about making any sounds or scaring the reindeer off.

"Like us?" Tredge asks.

'Question number one of a day of many,' thinks Yves.

"The herd of deer, grazing all around us, they wouldn't be grazing so close if they were afraid," Ultor tells them.

"Maybe they didn't see us, you think?" Tredge asks, still whispering.

"No, they see you. Reindeer have excellent instincts. They know you are here and that you mean them no harm." Ultor has seen these types of deer before in his travels. "Ya'll getting up today?" he asks them. He can tell this day will be clearer and better for traveling already. They can actually see the land that lay before them.

The three children get up with the eyes of the reindeer watching and begin to pack up their camp. As they are readying to leave, they see the reindeer turn and follow a trail. In the distance, there are people, farmers, herding them to a pasture. The local people, referred to as Greenlanders, herd the reindeer inland for the day to protect them from the cold.

Jotur stops packing and watches the Greenlanders. They aren't as savage or wild looking as in the stories she's heard. Their father often traveled to this region for trade and would return home with new trinkets and stories to share.

Yves seems to read her mind. "They don't look so wild," he whispers to his sister as he stuffs the last blanket into a satchel. They continue to watch the Greenlanders herd the deer, inching closer to their nearly packed camp.

"Yeah, I thought that too, but...," Jotur is speaking to her brother when the herders finally cross the boundary into their camp and, unbeknown to the Greenlanders, interrupt her. Jotur doesn't know if it is hostile or intentional. Yves, though he doesn't fully grab his sword, covers it with his hand.

"*Kveðja!*" one of the strangers says, speaking an Old Norse dialectal. He makes eye contact with Yves and tensely awaits a response; however, the children don't recognize this language. Being the eldest in the group, Ultor stands up from the stump he is perched upon, which startles the Greenlander, who apparently didn't see him. He first approached Yves, believing him to be the oldest male in the group. A few words are shared among Ultor and the Greenlander until they finally find a mutual dialect to understand. Surprisingly the language is one their mother had been trying to teach them, but they can only understand a few words as it had been a while. The Greenlander tells them that his people are descendants of Vikings that had traveled to the icy land before them long ago. They continue their discussion over breakfast, provided by the Greenlander. It is a treat for the children to sit with the Greenlander as his guest while Ultor translates.

"Where is their settlement?" Jotur asks, noticing no evidence of a settlement of the slightest kind in sight. Ultor explains to the children that The Greenlanders have adapted to the ways of the Inuit, another group of people inhabiting Greenland.

"They are nomadic now," Ultor says. "They follow the herds of deer and move from camp to camp. Right now, they are moving south for the winter." Ultor continues to relate the tale of the trolls that rampaged their village. The Greenlander, with much relief, reports that trolls are not a concern to them in this area, but they are in constant danger from wolves and polar bears. Tredge, relatively quiet despite the intriguing situation, soon interrupts with a question.

"Aren't you going to tell them about the Valkyries and our quest to find Asgard?" Tredge asks. Ultor is hoping to skip that part of the story, not knowing how the Greenlanders will react. Reluctantly, Ultor begins to explain the children's theory. The Greenlander, surprisingly supportive, says any journeys past this point will take the light from the day.

"Sun-less days?" Tredge questions, confused.

"Yes," Ultor confirms. "There is only night during the winter season, the sunlight will end, and we will have only darkness in which to travel."

"That will take forever," Tredge says. "...and it will be cold in the dark!" Brave little Tredge is still a bit frightened of the dark, though he wouldn't admit it, and he knows they have to continue north. After eating,

Ultor tells them that the Greenlander has a solution for the Vikings' dilemma of traveling in the dark and cold. He begins to herd up twelve reindeer and harnesses them together, then hitches them to the front of their boat.

"Now the boat can sled across the snow and ice with ease," Ultor says. As they start to bid their new friends farewell, Yves reaches in his shirt and pulls out his sailor's Lanyard, then walks over to the leader of the Greenlanders.

"This was given to me by my father. It was mined from the strongest iron in the land to represent strength. I want you to have it for the kindness you have shown us today," Yves tells them while Ultor translates again. Yves takes it off and lays it across the leader's hands, who holds it out to show the others. Yves continues, "…and as a symbol of your good faith and your hospitality." Yves looks at the others and smiles, taking the lanyard and simply draping it over the Greenlander's head. The Greenlander looks surprised and bows his head in thanks without looking up from the anchor lanyard. He seems very pleased.

"I don't think he has seen anything like it," Jotur says quietly to Tredge as the two watch off to the side. Yves bows to the leader then turns around and heads over to the harnessed reindeer. Tredge, Jotur, and Ultor follow close behind. Those were the last words spoken to the Greenlanders.

The Pack

Yves stands behind the head of the dragon at the hull of the ship, guiding the reindeer northward while

Jotur and the others take shelter from the cold. The sails are lowered and unhooked to provide an enclosure shielding them from the bitter winds. Ice slings up from the earth as the reindeer pull the boat across the snow. Even though they all wear their under-tunics made of linen, extra skins, and over-tunics of wool, the climate is fierce. The lowered sails help to offer additional shelter from the bitter chill. It is only a little past midday, but the sun is already beginning to set. Soon the days will see no sun at all, as the Greenlanders told them. Bifrost is again visible in the sky. Its vibrant colors tease them in their search.

The next few days are long, with each day providing shorter periods of light and extended periods of darkness. They often see herds of musk, oxen, and an occasional polar bear or two, but no settlers or any sign of human civilization. To help pass the time, Ultor begins telling more stories of his adventures as a young Viking. He is worried for the children's safety in this bitter cold, but he doesn't show it. At night, or when they need to rest since it seems to be nighttime more often, they sleep in the boat, taking turns at the hull. They keep from building fires for fear of the loss of firewood, attracting wild animals, or worse, trolls, even though no one would admit it. They aren't even sure trolls exist since all they have heard are stories about them, but they don't want to take any chances. In addition, fuel is a necessity in the north for survival, and it is already becoming scarce.

By the third night, Yves begins to let his guard down. He feels no need to stand at the front continuously, watching the nothingness. It is simply an endless time of staring into the darkness. Without a fire to attract anything, they all agree they are basically invisible in the dark landscape. On the fourth eve of their journey across the land, while they rest with no one on guard, they awake to a startling sound. The deer begin to scuffle in their places.

"Did ya'll hear that? Howling wolves?!" Yves says seriously, jumping up. "It's a pack!"

"Yves!" Ultor says harshly to get his attention away from the howling. "Yves, you take the stern," he says, handing him his sword.

He reaches to grab Jotur's bow and hands it to her. "Tredge, you got your axe?" Ultor asks, already knowing the answer. It never leaves the boy's side, he noticed earlier. He then grabs three torches and begins lighting them. Ultor hands one to Yves, then light another for Jotur and one for himself. As he jumps out of the boat, Yves follows closely behind, both with torches and swords in hand. Jotur, placing the oversized helmet on Tredge's head, looks gravely at Yves. Before he turns away, he mouths to her, 'You guard the ship.' She nods in agreement. Tredge stands right beside her, his axe in hand.

Ultor and Yves walk quietly around the front of the boat. Yves nudges Ultor, "There!" he points out a wolf not too far in the distance, showing it to Ultor.

"He is not alone," Ultor responds. "Stay sharp."

Ultor spots the second wolf just steps away from the first and puts his hand out for Yves to stop. The torches don't give them much light. If they can see them, the wolves are closer than they thought. They take a step together, closer to assess the pack. As far as Yves can tell, the group consists of three large females, one larger than the rest, pups they can only hear in the distance of the shadows, and one very large male. The wolves are distracted by something. They take another step closer together. The pack has a mother musk ox with her calf alone and surrounded.

"It's too dark to fight wolves," Yves tells Ultor. "I have an idea," he says, calling to his sister as quietly as possible. "Jotur, bring your bow." Knowing where the wolf pack is, he thinks Tredge will be safe on the boat, and his sister is the best shot with a bow. They are still standing between the wolves and the ship. Jotur carefully disembarks and walks up to join them, not taking her eyes off the pack. She reaches into her satchel, pulls out an arrow, and lights it on fire. Jotur knows exactly what Yves was thinking. They had pretended to light arrows all the time in their pretend battles, but this is for real. Once lit, Jotur pulls back on the bow, aims, and lets it go straight and swift. The arrow, released gently from her forefingers, flies like a streak of lightning across the sky. She hopes, at the least, it will scare the wolves away, but when the arrow comes down, it strikes the largest male in the hindquarters. Her heart is pounding.

"Good shot!" Tredge shouts from the boat.

"SHHHH!" Yves reminds him. It is obvious she hit one of the male wolves simply by his jerky motion and yelp from indescribable pain. One of the females in front of the group, obviously the alpha female, turns toward them and yells in anger.

"You should have minded your own business, humans! We would have left you alone, but now we will take your reindeer and then take you!" the wolf mother growls at them.

The Vikings look at one another as if to confirm they all heard the wolf's attack, but they have no time to discuss, for they have been spotted. The rest of the wolf pack follows their leader and turns from the musk oxen, charging at the boat and the twelve tied-up reindeer. Ultor leaps forward with his sword.

Jotur yells to Tredge, "Quickly, let's start a fire of burning timber, and it might help keep them away."

"Light the arrow tips on fire again!" Tredge tells her as he leaps from the boat with his short axe and torch.

"That was a lucky shot," she says, not believing she could do it again.

Ultor, still charging at the wolves, attacks the female wolf that still seems to be leading the pack. He now has a sword in one hand and a torch in the other, swinging both. Ultor fights hard. The wolf rears up on his hind legs and knocks Ultor to the ground. The rest of the wolf pack heads straight for the deer. Yves continues to back up in an effort to protect the deer and positions himself right in front of them.

"Hang on Ultor!" Jotur yells to him.

Tredge, now beside Jotur, begins to hand her burning arrows. As she carefully takes aim, she closes her left eye to line up the shot, then lets the arrow go into the sky, lighting up the night again. Jotur's shot strikes the wolf that has Ultor pinned to the ground and immediately sets her fur on fire. Letting out a big yelp, the wolf backs away from Ultor. The mother wolf, fearful and in pain, howls to her pack and runs off into the darkness. The others quickly follow her and disappear into the night. The stench of her burning fur lingers in the cold air. Ultor looks over to Jotur to say thank you with a smile on his face. Feeling proud of her and the boys, Ultor thinks to himself, *'They have now survived their first battle and with it a tale of their own to tell.'*

"Look!" Tredge shouts, pointing for Ultor, Jotur, and Yves to turn and see a herd of ox stepping out of hiding, one by one. The mother ox and her calf scurry back and hide behind the herd. The Vikings smile at their success.

"There must be thousands," Tredge says, exaggerating a bit. "That's a lot of those…mooses."

"Oxen, and it is definitely a large herd," Yves confirms.

"The calf and mother must have been separated from the rest. The wolves would have never attacked a strong herd of that size," Ultor explains.

"Aaghhh, I think they are coming this way," Tredge notices. The four members of the small Viking clan stand motionless as the herd of oxen comes closer toward the boat. Each one stands in amazement at the sight which lies before them. The herd stops short of their ship, and the mother Oxen, her calf still close to her side, and a large bull proceed to come forth. The mother speaks first in a soft voice, still trembling from the attack.

"Thank you," she mutters to the Vikings. "I became separated from the herd when my calf wandered off, and I went in search of him alone." The bull then speaks up and addresses the Viking children.

"We are in debt to you, for I am the leader of this herd, and our calf will someday grow up to follow in my footsteps. We are moving south before the day and night become one, and there is endless darkness. There is no place to graze now. It is all dead ahead. There is nothing here for you in the north. Why are you traveling this way?"

Yves speaks up, "We seek the rainbow bridge Bifrost to reach Asgard so we can return our parents to our home."

"They were taken from us by mistake," Tredge adds.

"Good luck to you then. You must journey beyond lands' end," the bull replies, "for I have been to the edge of this land, and no bridge lies upon it."

And with those words, the herd turns from the Vikings and departs, moving south. "It is still early in the morning and darkness all around. I think we will see the sun no more," Ultor says indifferently as if talking to the leader of an oxen herd is normal. "It is best that we begin to move onward. We are still several days' time from the northern coast."

Brodnak

It takes four more days until they come to the sea again, but it does not look at all like the seas they left on the other side of the land. This sea is covered with chunks of ice of all sizes, floating everywhere. Day and night no longer hold any meaning for the Vikings, for it is now dark at all times. They decide to set their camp on the land one more time before casting off into the frozen sea. They tie the reindeer up for one last night before letting them go, thinking they will still need them when they wake to help launch their boat back into the water. Ultor and Yves prepare the fire for camp and start working on a hot meal to warm them up. Jotur and Tredge walk the coastline, trying to find a small hill from which to slide the boat back into the sea. They walk for nearly thirty minutes in the dark, almost accustomed to it now, before Tredge notices a small step up in the sand in his footing below.

"I think I see a mound over here by the seashore," Tredge points out the direction.

"Can't see anything yet," Jotur says. "We will have to go a little further to make sure." A few more steps, and she, too, can feel the ground beginning to rise, making a slight incline.

"We must be sure that this place is steep enough for the reindeer to pull the boat up on top," she explains to Tredge, "…and then we can push the boat into the water." As they get closer to the hill, their eyes begin to focus on the mound, and they begin to hear muffled sounds.

"It sounds like the hill is breathing heavily," Tredge tells his sister, but she pays him no attention.

"We must climb to the top and see if it is suitable for launching the boat," Jotur says, focusing on the task at hand. She is cold and wants to return to camp and the fire. "It is probably just the shoreline. It sounds different with the big pieces of ice in the water," she explains, but as they walk closer, she hears something too. The noise is becoming louder and easier to interpret.

"No, it still sounds like breathing," Tredge confirms, "...and it sounds rather strained," he points out.

Jotur, beginning to feel guilty for brushing off her brother, stops to listen. "I hear something, but I doubt it is breathing," she whispers. "Tredge, get behind me."

They continue slowly, together now. When they reach the bottom of the hill, the breathing sound continues, but they can't seem to find a source.

"Okay, okay, I think it does sound a lot like breathing," Jotur concedes to her brother. She begins to step up the hill, but to her surprise, it doesn't feel like the ground. It is too soft beneath her feet. Tredge follows her steps. At that very moment, a great voice booms.

"WHO TREADS ON ME?" the voice says to them.

Jotur and Tredge step back in astonishment. They make no answer. Again the voice asks, this time a bit less loud and confrontational.

"WHO TREADS ON ME?" the voice repeats itself.

Jotur answers, "Two Vikings. I am Jotur, and this is my brother Tredge. We seek Asgard by way of Bifrost and, more immediately, a small hill from which to launch our boat. Now who asks of us who we are?" she says bravely, not knowing why she told the voice where they are headed.

The hill answers, "I am no hill, Viking Jotur. Can Vikings not discern a hill from a whale?"

"It's a whale! It's a Whale!" Tredge exclaims, jumping up and down in excitement. He had never seen a whale, let alone stood on one.

"Stop jumping!" the voice cries out.

"Oh, sorry!" Tredge tells the voice and immediately stops.

"We may tell one from the other in the light or if the hill is on land and the whale in the sea. How is it that you are on land?" asks Jotur.

"My Name is Brodnak. I am stranded here," the whale says, "and cannot return to the sea. I accidentally beached myself laughing at a burning wolf trying to enter the sea. Wolves cannot swim, you know, and I did not want his filthy hide in the water, so I splashed to blow water on the wolf, thinking I was helping, but I misjudged the distance in the dark and fell upon the shoreline. So now I am stranded," Brodnak confesses to the two little Vikings.

"Ha ha ha! My sister set the wolf ablaze with a flaming arrow," Tredge laughs, excited to tell the whale. "It attacked our reindeer, and we rescued a musk ox and her calf from the whole pack."

The whale laughs heartily and then says, "The humor which you have provided me is great, but at a great cost, for I fear if I cannot return to the water, I will certainly die. I am too exhausted now from the struggle to continue trying."

"Maybe we can help you," Yves says, appearing seemingly out of nowhere and stepping onto the hill… whale. He had gone looking for his brother and sister along the coast when they had not returned to the camp promptly.

"And who might you be?" The whale Brodnak asks.

"I'm Yves, her other brother," he answers.

"How many brothers do you have?" The whale questions.

"Only the two," Jotur answers. "Two is enough."

Yves has an idea. He thinks they can both help each other get back into the water. "Can you survive through the night hours?" he asks.

"Yes, since there will be no sun, I can survive for many hours, but breathing is very hard, and I will be at the mercy of the wolves if they return," replies Brodnak.

"Then I will stay here and protect you," says Yves. "Tredge, you must return to the camp and bring Ultor. Pack up our things too. We will camp here."

Tredge runs the whole distance back to the boat, with Jotur following at her own pace. In his excitement to tell Ultor about their find, he is not watching his step in the icy darkness, but luckily he is light on his feet and sticks to the shoreline. When he gets back to their camp, Tredge immediately starts talking nonstop as Ultor tries to listen intensely.

"... and we heard a voice, and we were stepping on him...," he says, panting in the process from both his excitement and running.

"...and his name is Brodnak," he says. "He's huge, and he needs our help." Tredge explains how the whale is stuck on the shore, about the burning arrow and the wolves returning, all the while packing up the camp to move. Ultor and Jotur quickly harness the reindeer and head down the shoreline with their boat. Ultor can't wait to meet this whale called Brodnak.

"This is our elder, Ultor," Tredge says, politely introducing their friend as if they weren't standing on the icy cold shoreline of the North talking to a giant whale.

"Nice to meet you," Ultor says, slightly shocked at the truth of Tredge's story. "Now, do you have any idea how we can get you back into the sea?" he asks.

"No, as I'm sure they have told you, I beached myself and cannot move anymore from trying," Brodnak tells Ultor.

"Well, we can set up camp, light a fire and protect you in the night," Ultor suggests. "And meanwhile, maybe we can think of something." With that said, he starts to unpack again while Yves starts on the fire.

Once they are all gathered around the fire, they start sharing their ideas on how to get Brodnak back into the sea. They sit just a few yards away from Brodnak, so the fire can't reach him, but he can still hear the discussion.

"What if we harness him to the reindeer," Yves suggests.

"Not a bad idea," Brodnak confirms.

"Yeah, we can drag him to a hillside and slide him off into the sea," Tredge adds with eagerness as what he thinks would be fun for Brodnak.

"Okay, not such a good idea," Brodnak vetoes it fast. "Plus, there are no hills close by."

"Good point," Tredge replies, not realizing that in his master plan.

Eventually, the Vikings settle on the idea of building mounds from the snow and ice and using the great oars of the boat to lift and move him a little at a time, hoping he will slide a little to help. They all work through the night hours, and finally, after moving Brodnak a few inches at a time, they are able to slip him into the water!

Brodnak disappears immediately into the cold sea. Suddenly, a moderate distance from the shore, the whale breaches the water's surface in a magnificent leap. He then returns close to the edge of the ice-covered land and thanks the Vikings.

"Many, many thanks," he says. "Is there any way I may help you?" he asks. "I am forever in your debt, but I do have one question for you. Why are Vikings sailing a boat across these dark winters?"

Ultor answers, "We sailed too far west on our journey, and the wind trapped us against the land, so we have traveled over the land to reach this part of the sea. We are now stranded as you were, for we can't move our boat back into the water."

"That is no trouble for me," says Brodnak. "I can easily pull your boat into the waters. Rest now, though; refresh yourselves, as will I, and we will begin tomorrow." Brodnak explains his plan, saying that he needs to swim and get stronger before he can pull their ship into the water.

"When you are ready, just slap the water three times with your ship's oar or your hand, and I will hear you and return to you," Brodnak says, and with that, he submerges into the icy water. The Vikings quickly prepare their supper, eat, and fall fast asleep, exhausted from the excitement of the day.

Sea Bound

The Vikings awake refreshed, ready to embark from the icy land. All four are looking forward to getting back on the sea. Ultor and Jotur begin to make all the preparations. They untie the sails and refold them appropriately. Though they will miss the shelter they provide against the harsh winds; they will undoubtedly need them on the sea. Yves tends to the reindeer with Tredge. They both untie the reindeer, bidding them a thank you, and send them southward so they can rejoin their herd.

"What time is it?" Tredge asks. He is obsessed with knowing the time of day since it is always dark now.

"Half past a freckle and a hair," Ultor says, overhearing his question.

Tredge doesn't get his humor. "What's that mean?" he replies, confused.

"It means you're asking too many questions!" Ultor says with a wink this time. "Honestly, I don't know what it means; it's something my mom would say to me when I kept asking her the same question. It's close to noontime, I think."

The darkness provides no reference to daytime, so they eat a meager breakfast for lunch. Afterward, when they've finished packing up, Yves steps onto the shoreline and slaps the water's surface three times with the boat oars. In only a matter of minutes, Brodnak appears in the distance and blows a great blast of water from his blowhole.

"Secure a long line to your boat," shouts Brodnak, "and cast the loose end into the water." When everyone is secure, Brodnak grabs the rope's end in his great mouth and swims away from the shore. The rope becomes taut, and the boat surges forward, splashing into the icy sea. Brodnak pulls the boat with amazing ease, the same ship that the Vikings couldn't have budged even if they tried. Brodnak swims back to the boat and bids the Vikings a goodbye. He reminds them that he is forever in their debt, and they need only to slap the surface of the water three times, and he will recognize their call. At that, Brodnak says, "Farewell!" and disappears under the water once again.

Finally, they have returned to the sea. The Vikings need their sail to propel and maneuver the boat. Their temporary shelter is torn down, and the sails are put back in place. Yves rolls up the sail about halfway so it will not be torn from the bitter wind. The partial sails drive the boat steadily against the ice-covered sea, but it can't proceed very fast due to the ice chunks in the water.

"You must always assume that the ice you see is just the tip of what lies below," Ultor tells Tredge, feeling good again being on the sea. He is pleasantly surprised at how much he enjoys the young Vikings' company. He has forgotten about finding them a home with another Viking clan and is starting to actually believe in the children's quest.

"So, these icebergs are just peaks?" Tredge asks.

"Some of them, but do you want to take a chance by guessing which ones?" Ultor questions him.

"What if we guess wrong," Tredge asks.

"Well, if we go too close, too fast, they could rip a hole in the boat and sink us," Yves chips in, ever so positively.

"Sink us?" Tredge asks, afraid of sinking in the cold waters. "We'll go slowly; I'll keep watch!" Tredge is serious now as he sits at the boat's edge, peering into the sea. The prow of the ship is designed to break through the pieces of ice slowly; however, from time to time, they would have to get out and chop the ice with their axes and swords to keep moving. Their travel time is slow as the boat becomes lodged in the ice often. During the last few hours, clouds form overhead, and snow begins to fall. It is also getting colder, making them think it is nightfall, but with no stars or landmarks, the water and ice all look the same.

***

Sleep falls on each of the young Vikings for a while. When they awake, they guess it is morning, but it is still snowing and as dark as any night.

"It's easy to lose your direction under these conditions," Ultor says, noticing Tredge is waking up. He was supposed to be keeping watch.

"And I can't see Bifrost with the cloud hovering over us," Tredge exclaims in disappointment.

"I think we will just have to guess at our direction," Yves tells Tredge as he rolls over and stretches. The boat stops again. The hull is frozen to an ice pack, and Ultor immediately goes to work. Yves, noticing the large piece of ice Ultor is trying to destroy, exits the boat and starts chopping too. Yves carefully watches his footing and looks around to make sure he doesn't slip into the dark waters. As he surveys the iceberg, he can't seem to locate its edges.

"Can we go around?" he questions Ultor.

"I don't know; I didn't check." Ultor realizes he hadn't surveyed the iceberg before picking away at it.

"I think we are surrounded," Yves says, carefully taking another step outward from the boat.

"Surrounded?" Ultor questions. "Surrounded by water," he jokes.

"No, seriously; I mean surrounded by ice," Yves says as he looks up at Ultor, who is not understanding. "The boat seems to be suddenly amidst a sea of solid ice. We're wedged in."

"I guess with the rapidly falling temperatures, ice has formed all around the boat this time," Ultor says, the only explanation he can think of.

"How will we ever free the boat now?" Tredge asks as he inspects the boat's edges encased in ice. Jotur is up now to wonder what all the commotion is about.

"There is no freeing the boat?" Jotur asks.

"No, we will have to travel on foot," Ultor says.

It is not the answer Jotur wants. "Well, let's carry what provisions we can," she tells the boys as she begins to pack up. *'I was just getting used to being back in the boat,'* she thinks to herself.

"Can we not signal Brodnak?" Tredge asks.

"We are surrounded by ice, not water," Yves says, frustrated he doesn't know the answers to some of his own questions.

"I'm sure he is mighty enough to break through the ice," Tredge believes.

"He is mighty indeed," replies Jotur, "but we cannot break through to the water to signal him. Ultor is right.

We will have to continue our journey on foot. Gather as much as you can carry and bring only the essentials."

They all gather their gear and start to leave the boat. Ultor decides which way he thinks is north, guessing from his memory of the last time they saw the stars and Bifrost, and they all head in that direction. After walking over the ice for what seems like ages, Tredge notices that the snow isn't coming straight down anymore but rather swirling about them.

"Hey, look!" he says, drawing everyone's attention. "It's stopped snowing, yet I still see it coming down. It's not reaching me, though."

"Yeah, we're under a cloud," Yves states without looking up.

"Well, that doesn't make any sense. Snow comes from clouds," Jotur explains.

"Hey, I can see the stars too!" Tredge points out. They all look up to see that they aren't under a cloud. Instead, they are walking under an area with a clear circle of sky in the middle of the clouds.

"No, we are entering a clear zone of some type," he says, not really understanding why it isn't snowing on them or why there is a perfectly clear circle among the clouds. They have all stopped walking and are gazing up at the stars through the opening.

Tredge suddenly exclaims, "Bifrost, Bifrost, there it is!" Sure enough, there, in the middle of the clearing in the clouds, is the rainbow bridge of legend.

"I can't believe it," Ultor says in disbelief. "Impossible."

The bridge can be seen when the snow swirls just the right way and the light of the stars shine in the same spot. The four Vikings run from spot to spot where they see the snow swirling, but by the time they get there, they see no bridge.

"I know this is where I saw the bridge," says Tredge.

"Yes, it touches right here," agrees Jotur. "I saw it too."

Yves reaches down to the ground and picks up a handful of loose snow. He tosses it into the air, and as it falls, some of the snow never reaches the ground.

"There!" he says, "There is the bridge! We can only see it as the snow passes over it." Ultor simply grins and laughs to himself at the ingenuity and cleverness of Yves. The others quickly throw more and more snow onto it, fascinated by its magic.

"How can we climb it if we can't see it?" asks Tredge. "We can't carry enough snow to cover the whole thing."

Ultor has been silent during their conversation, and the children think he is just walking in circles. However, Ultor has been walking around the base of the bridge.

"We can see the bridge, but only if we look straight at it and not through it. You must position yourself to see it at just the right angle," Ultor tells them as he is still studying the sight before him.

The three children move around to where Ultor stands, and suddenly Bifrost appears to them all. The children start laughing in delight that they have found the infamous bridge. Ultor watches the children dancing around in the snow and cheering. He is becoming very fond of these young Vikings. They have become his new family, and he treasures them as they do him now.

CHAPTER III

THE CROSSROADS
• • • • • • • • • • • • • • •

Bifrost

"What are we waiting for?" Tredge asks. "Let's go!" He takes the first step onto the bridge. Jotur's hand quickly grabs his arm holding him back from his second step. As Tredge struggles to free himself from his sister's grasp, she explains.

"Wait, don't you remember your lessons about the gods?" She recalls that Bifrost is protected by Heimdall, a guardian of the gods.

"He's only nine," Yves reminds her.

"Nine and a half!" Tredge corrects him. "…and I do know my gods! Heimdall has a castle which lies upon the summit of Bifrost, called Homeburk."

"Himinbjorg," Yves corrects him. "…and not nine and a half yet!"

"...And you want to make it to ten, don't you?" Jotur says in a more serious tone. "Heimdall has excellent hearing and sight."

"Yeah, yeah. I know," Tredge says, wishing they would stop worrying about him so much. He is ready to get going.

"Well, did you know he can hear the grass grow and see for hundreds of miles and that he never sleeps?" Yves shares with him.

"Oh," is all Tredge replies. Heimdall didn't seem so terrifying in the stories, but now the thought of crossing his bridge with him watching does seem a bit scary.

"Just stay close to us," Jotur tells him as she steps closer to Tredge.

"...And tread carefully and watch for his castle," Yves says, thinking it will convince him to watch his step and keep quiet for a bit. He then looks over at Jotur to give her the go-ahead to start walking. She takes a deep breath and takes a step with Tredge by her side.

"So, he can't sleep, or he won't sleep?" Tredge asks, "...and what does grass growing sound like?"

"Treeeddggee," his sister looks at him sternly. "Now is not the time for your questions. And if he can hear the grass grow, he will definitely hear you if you don't stop with your questions!"

'When is ever a time for my questions?' he wonders. Nevertheless, he respects his sister's request and remains quiet for the time being, distracted by the mystical bridge.

As they begin their ascent on Bifrost, they notice that the bridge is easily seen once upon it. They all try to move quietly but inevitably make some noise. Ultor's armor clangs with each step he takes, no matter how slow and stealthily he moves. With weary legs and conscious of the racket he makes, he falls behind. The climb is steep at first, but after a few hours, the ascent tapers off. As the slope tapers, the air thins, but this has little to no effect on the young, healthy Vikings. It is obvious, however, that breathing is becoming more of a struggle for Ultor. The children continue to climb steadily, having youth and vitality on their side but looking back every so often to see if Ultor is okay. As they begin to reach the pinnacle, the air around them becomes thick with moisture, and they find themselves among a haze of a cloud-like vapor.

"Everyone, watch your step," Jotur says to the boys realizing their sight is becoming obscured.

"I can see fine," Tredge tells his sister, "Can't you?"

Jotur doesn't respond but just keeps her eyes on her footing. She knows Tredge and Yves will be okay and tells them to watch their step more for Ultor's benefit, not realizing he has fallen farther behind out of the range of their voices. Being of unstable footing, he could easily lose his balance even without the haze.

After climbing through the foggy atmosphere for some time, the haze begins to disperse slightly, allowing light to fall upon their pathway. The light gradually seeps back in until the misty haze is lifted, and the Vikings can see they are above the clouds. The light makes Tredge rubs his eyes as the other two walk on, squinting. As their eyes adjust, they begin to recognize that the world has unfolded beneath them.

"We can rest here," Jotur says as she stops just short of the bridge's peak, realizing Ultor is nowhere in sight. "We need to have some water."

"Good idea!" Yves plops down with no regard for where he is and covers his eyes. They have traveled through darkness for many days and nights, and the young Vikings are beginning to feel tired. As Jotur grabs her canteen and begins to take a sip, she notices the beautiful sights down below.

"Yves, come look!" she says, astonished with what she sees. She looks out across all the land, able to see for miles. She rests her hands upon her hips and just stands there for a few minutes.

"What a sight!" she says to herself aloud.

Despite needing his rest, Yves gets up and walks over to Jotur.

"This better be worth it," he groans.

"What? What?" Tredge runs over and pushes himself between them, "What is it?" He is never subtle.

The three stand there looking at the splendor of the land below them, speechless. Land and seas beneath them spread out like a feast upon the earth. Rivers like snakes, rolling hills of grasslands, frozen plains, and sand and sea are all set before them. The same light that falls upon their face also falls upon the distant lands that exist beyond the borders of their knowledge. Eventually, Yves breaks the silence.

"We'll let Ultor catch up and regain his breath, and then we can go on together." Yves estimates he is at least an hour behind them.

"Where are we?" Tredge asks, "In heaven?"

"We are definitely not in our world anymore," Yves says, not having seen anything like it before.

"Is this Asgard?" Tredge asks, but the older two don't know either.

"Honestly, I don't know," Jotur admits. "I think it is still Bifrost."

"This is the longest bridge ever," Tredge notes.

They try to rest their eyes, but they have traveled in the darkness for so long that the sky seems very bright, and the grandeur of the heavens is mesmerizing. Tredge, in spite of the light, falls fast asleep.

The Castle of Heimdall

Jotur and Yves begin to hear a slight clanging noise coming from behind them. A shadow begins to appear through the misty fog and eventually into the light. The steps are constant as a ticking clock.

"Clang, clang, clang," the noise continues in perfect timing. The blurry figure becomes sharper, and there appears Ultor. Jotur gets up and runs to hug him as he smiles in delight to catch up with them. They don't tell him they have been waiting two hours for him. After letting Ultor rest, they wake Tredge up from his peaceful nap and continue on their journey.

"Are we still on Bifrost?" Tredge asks, a bit groggy from his nap.

"Yes, we are definitely still on Bifrost. We haven't moved! What do you think we just carried you?" Yves sarcastically remarks. It isn't long until they reach the peak of Bifrost. There they can see the great castle that lay upon it at the top of the highest point.

"That must be Heimdall's Great Hall," whispers Yves stating the obvious he thinks.

Jotur encourages them to keep moving, "Well, we must be getting close." She doesn't want to stop, hoping they can get past the castle without notice.

"Yeah! We're getting closer to the end," Tredge exclaims quietly, happy to think they will soon be done walking or climbing up for a while.

"No," Yves corrects him, "it still looks at least a mile away until we reach the castle, and that would be only halfway to Asgard," or so he logically thinks.

"Halfway? Aaghhh!" Tredge says in disbelief.

They continue to walk, each one keeping an eye on the castle, expecting Heimdall, the keeper of the realm, to fly out at any moment in vengeance.

When they finally reach the pinnacle of Bifrost, they can see all across the land below them. Ultor is amazed by the sight of the world below and begins to point out their journey, like marking it on a live map.

"Look, right there, see the waters which lie southward? That's the freezing sea we crossed with the bitter winds. And here, over here," he points to show Tredge, who is listening to him intensely, "…and that's where we met the wolf pack."

"Don't remind me," Tredge says, shaking his head. He looks over his shoulder. "And that's the shoreline where we met Brodnak," he points for Ultor to see this time.

Yves jumps in, "And what about that mist or dew? Where did it go?" he asks.

"The trees look so small too," Tredge points out to a forest not far below them.

"Yeah, kind of makes us look rather small to the gods, I bet," Jotur thinks out loud.

"And insignificant," Yves concludes.

"Ultor, how come we can see down from Bifrost, but when we were down there, we couldn't see up here?" Tredge wonders.

"I bet it's like a window of some kind where you can't see in from Midgard, but you can see out on Bifrost." It sounds like a good enough theory for boys, Ultor thinks.

"Yeah, the gods have to see out to watch us," Yves teases Tredge. "To see your silly face and laugh." Tredge tackles Yves, and the two begin to wrestle like they used to do every day before the trolls' invasion.

Jotur watches the boys and Ultor as they relive their journey thus far. She can't decide who is more excited, Tredge, Yves, or Ultor, and smiles for the first time in weeks. She then turns and starts walking ahead of them, taking the lead. After a few steps, she rounds the peak, looks up, and then stops in her tracks. She has been so entertained by the boys she forgets to look ahead. She let her guard down, and there right in front of her, stands Himinbjorg, the castle.

"Quiet everyone," she whispers, putting her hands out as if to stop them physically from making any noise. One by one, the Vikings turn around and have the same gut-wrenching reaction. They know if the castle is there, and it is real, then so is Heimdall. The god was born of nine mothers and possesses an acute sense of sight, hearing, and knowledge.

"What, what is it?" Tredge asks, not paying attention to his sister's gestures. "Why are we stopping?"

"It's the castle of Heimdall," Jotur answers. "Now hush, or he will hear us!"

"Okay!" Tredge says as he leans over to Ultor. "I hope I get to see his horse," he says quietly. He thinks out loud, *'I've heard it has a golden mane!'*

"Shush, don't speak out loud. He'll hear you!" Jotur stresses, waving her arms at them now.

"Gull topper," Ultor mumbles as Jotur motions for him to shush too.

"If Heimdall hears us, he will surely cast us from the bridge, then what will we do?" whispers Jotur. "We must proceed as quietly as possible."

"Start over?!" Tredge whispers to Ultor.

The Gothic structure sits on the highest peak just beside the Bifrost Bridge, which it guards. The castle is quite enchanting, made of gray limestone and black marble. As the four Vikings pass by, it is hard not to look in appreciation of such beauty.

'Absolutely stunning,' thinks Jotur as she walks by quietly, looking up at the intimidating structure. *'No wonder it is called the castle in the heavens.'*

"Hey Yves, if Heimdall hears us and comes out and casts us from the bridge, will he cast us all the way back home or just off the bridge?" Tredge can't help his curiosity.

"Shuuuush," Yves agrees with Jotur. "It's best not to find out. Do you want to be killed?"

"Killed? Or did you say tossed?" Tredge snaps back, getting worried now. "Jotur said *tossed* from the bridge."

"No, actually, she said *cast* from the bridge, not tossed," Yves corrects him. A favorite game of theirs.

"Seriously, now you want to be specific? I don't know what he will do. No one has ever been found on Bifrost or has ever tried to cross the bridge as far as I know, and if they did, it isn't in any of the history books we read." She is beginning to raise her voice. "Now, pay attention!" With that said, she turns and walks toward Ultor to check on him. He is starting to lag behind again, and Tredge has moved on to questioning Yves. Tredge looks at his older brother, annoyed at his sister's lecturing.

"It was just a question," Tredge whispers. Yves smiles at Tredge's innocence, though he begins to wonder himself if they would be sent back home or killed. He never realized before that this journey could bring them even more tragedy and grief. He just lost his parents, and he didn't want to lose his sister or brother too. As they slowly and stealthily pass under the shadow of Himinbjorg, there is no sign of movement but their own. There is no sight of the castle's master, Heimdall, so they creep on.

Once they pass the castle, they can finally see the full splendor of Asgard come into view and see the end of the rainbow bridge. Sure enough, at its end stands another huge castle, and beyond it, they can see the tips of other castles, their bases hidden by the beautiful scenery of flowers, trees, and green pastures. Nonetheless, Asgard is in sight. They walk toward the gates of Asgard, amazed at its beauty, jaws agape with astonishment.

Suddenly, without warning, the four Vikings hear screeching and look up. Before they know it, they are surrounded by Valkyries with no place to run. Swords are drawn, and bows pulled taught with arrows, ready to pierce their hearts with any sudden movement.

"Stop and announce yourself," one of the Valkyries states.

"Announce yourself?" Tredge questions in a whisper to his brother and sister. *'What does that mean,'* he ponders.

Jotur shields Tredge by reaching out her hand and sliding him partially behind her. This time he doesn't argue or ask why. Though they were asked to announce themselves, the Vikings aren't given a chance to respond. The Valkyries suddenly grab them, all of them, in one swift swoop, and before they know it, they are flying high over Bifrost.

Tredge wonders how high they can fly because they were already in the sky when they grabbed them. He doesn't ask. He is amazed by the sights below him, everything getting smaller and smaller. As he watches, he forgets to look for Yves, Jotur, and Ultor, who have just been taken captive too. His heart is racing, though he isn't as scared as he is mesmerized by the size of the trees and animals from such a height. His mind fills with questions. Yves is just as astonished to be flying. He can't believe he is riding with the Valkyries. He stares at them, memorizing their expressions and their movements. Yves wants to reach out and touch them, stroke their hair, but he realizes he can't move. He is bound somehow. Ultor is excited he is going to see Asgard and that he is finally being taken by the Valkyries. It doesn't occur to him that he is still alive and trespassing. Jotur, on the other hand, understands exactly what is happening, and she is frightened. They are in serious trouble.

"What are you doing with us?" shouts Jotur. "Put us down!" she demands, realizing that might not have been the right choice of words as she looks down from her flight.

"We are taking you before Odin, who shall decide your fate for entering Asgard," one of the Valkyries responds.

'*They speak*,' Jotur thinks to herself.

The Valkyries fly the four Vikings to the most extraordinary castle in all of Asgard and descend through its gate. The Valkyries, who transport their prisoners, dismount their steeds, and as they do, a fifth Valkyrie appears, presumably their leader. Only the leader continues onward as the others remain outside the grand structure. The three little Vikings, the elder Viking, and the leader of the Valkyries march together into a large hall, which has but one seat on the opposite end from the entrance and is surrounded by an audience. In the seat sits Odin, the leader of the gods. Tredge, quiet for far too long, whispers, "We're in for it now."

The Leader of the Gods

As the Vikings near the end of the hall, they see Odin sitting on an enormous and very ornate throne. Beside Odin sit his two wolves, Geri and Freki, and on the back of his seat sit his two ravens, Hugin and Munin. Odin himself has a long gray beard and wears a patch over one side of his face to cover a missing eye. He is clothed with a long cloak and holds a great spear.

'*He looks very god-like,*' Yves thinks to himself. When the Valkyrie leader approaches Odin, he sits straight up. His interest peeks with curiosity, for they never come to see him unless something is afoot.

"Brynhild," Odin's deep voice carries throughout the arena. Tredge, now a bit scared, steps just a bit closer to Yves and Jotur.

"My thanks for bringing these intruders to me," Odin expresses to Brynhild. The people in the crowd are halfway listening and are now beginning to notice the little strangers brought before Odin. "You may leave them to me now. Go and bring Heimdall to me so that I may know how these mortals passed by his guard on Bifrost."

"I hope we didn't get anyone in trouble," Tredge says, worrying about Heimdall. "Are WE in trouble?" he asks.

"Yeah, we are in serious trouble," Yves whispers to Tredge, not joking. "Now quit with the questions before you get us in more trouble." Tredge listens and quickly shifts to position himself between Jotur and Ultor, feeling safer.

Before Brynhild returns with Heimdall, the hall fills with many other gods, goddesses, dwarfs, elves, and giants. Tredge and Yves are beside themselves, gazing around at the characters from their storybooks coming to life.

"Tredge, look! There...it's Balder, Odin's second son! Now, what is he the god of?" he asks his younger brother in excitement, just like he used to quiz him in the old achieves at home.

"The god of love, peace, forgiveness, and justice!" Tredge says back proudly. "Forgiveness...we're going to need some of that!" he adds.

"And there, who is that?" Yves asks, pointing to his left.

"That's, that's...," Tredge closes his eyes, thinking. "...Oh, that's Hodr, his twin brother of darkness." He opens his eyes and smiles back at Yves. "Give me another, give me another!" he shouts at Yves, pulling on his arm, getting too loud.

"Her!" Yves points at a beautiful goddess.

"Freya, the goddess of love, fertility, and beauty," Tredge answers. "That was easy. Another! Another!" he asks again.

Jotur interrupts their little game, "And you left out the part where Freya is also the goddess of death and *shut up or you're going to get us all killed*!" she snaps with her great sense of sarcasm. "Do you not realize this is serious?"

"Yes, but look! We are surrounded by gods," Yves argues. "...plus we are like children to them, and they can't really hear us. Look, they are smiling at us." And for a moment, it did help them forget about their dire circumstances.

"Uh, we ARE children," Tredge corrects him. "Look, there's Loki!" His attention turns toward the throne of

Odin. "He's my favorite! He's right behind all those gods talking to Odin. I wonder what he's doing."

"Of course, the god of cunningness and mischief is your favorite!" Yves says as he pats him on the head, messing up his hair. The guards don't seem too happy with their roughhousing. Taking the hint, Yves stops. He knows his sister is right. They are in serious trouble.

***

The Viking children can't help but feel intimidated by such a crowd. And the more that enter the hall, the more insignificant they feel.

'Is this all on our behalf, because of us? Did we cause this gathering?' Tredge wonders. He stands there, silent now, naming the gods in his head one by one. There are also many other Asgardians besides gods standing around. Tredge sees an eight-legged horse next to some dwarfs. He wonders if those are the dwarfs who forged Thor's magic hammer. Time seems to stand still as Odin converses with a few of his advisors, obviously about the little Vikings as they keep looking down at them and then returning to their discussion. Just as the children and Ultor are paying close attention to the Asgardians, they, too, are being watched. The gods are very curious about these four Vikings who have entered the kingdom uninvited. The walls had never been breached before, and the news of the intruders is spreading fast.

Brynhild returns with Heimdall, and the guards announce their arrival to Odin. He immediately demands the crowd to hush by stomping his foot once, focusing his attention on the entrance of the hall. When Heimdall walks into the throne room, he is adorned in stunning white armor.

'It makes him even more striking for one so handsome,' thinks Jotur. Heimdall is considered one of the wisest gods in Asgard and is well respected. His presence alone has the crowd's immediate attention as everyone turns to admire him. The crowd parts for Heimdall to approach Odin, knowing that being summoned isn't good, especially after hearing of the intruders. Odin watches as his beloved Heimdall approaches his throne, more curious than angry about how these Vikings, a few children and an old man, for that fact, were not seen crossing Bifrost.

Heimdall reaches Odin and bows as he waits for Odin to speak first. Odin stands up and motions for him to come to him. It is custom not to approach Odin unless he requests or gestures you to do so. Heimdall stands up and walks to Odin but humbly keeps his head bowed as he approaches the throne, giving all authority to Odin. Odin doesn't waste any time; he gets right to the point.

"How is it that these four mortals have passed by your guard?" Odin says with all looking on.

Heimdall, fearing Odin's wrath, knows better than to lie; however, he also doesn't want to admit he was resting his eyes for just a second. Apparently, the story that Heimdall never sleeps is not altogether true; it just helps keep trespassers away.

"Odin, my great apologies," he says as he kneels again, this time directly in front of the divine god, bowing his head in respect. "I don't understand how they got past me. I felt no threat, heard no steps upon the bridge. I have watched for centuries, and no giant has passed."

Odin, taken aback that they could pass such a fierce guardian as Heimdall, doesn't know how to handle the intrusion. Heimdall is impassable, or so he thought, everyone thought.

"If mere children and an old man can pass you, then why not giants?" Odin asks, beginning to doubt Heimdall's ability to guard the bridge.

The queen speaks, who rarely interceded on such matters.

"Perhaps the fact they ARE children is the key to their passage." She pauses, looking for Odin's reaction. He looks at her, intrigued. His wife, the queen, Frigg, is adored by her husband and all of Asgard. She is always seen by Odin's side in every book, in every painting, and on every tapestry the children have ever seen. He loves and respects her. He bids her to continue.

"Heimdall has guarded us for ages and always protects us from the invasion of giants, so it is written, but nowhere do the writings say he is to protect us from children." She makes a good point. "Perhaps their innocence is the key to the kingdom."

"Very wise, Frigg," Odin replies, pleased with her reasoning.

"Well, so be it," Odin says to Heimdall. "Go figure out how we can now protect ourselves from children! I need to address these little Vikings and their intrusion!" And with a wave of his hand, Heimdall is dismissed and he turns to leave, relieved that he did not see the wrath of Odin today. Though, he too is curious about these Vikings that slipped past his castle, and so he stays. Heimdall merges into the crowd to watch the events unfold and tries to remain hidden.

Odin once again takes his seat on the throne and turns his attention to the Vikings who stand a few yards away, now guarded by three Asgardians.

"Come here," he demands.

Already knowing what he is about to ask and afraid he won't like the answer, the three Viking children step forward, with Jotur taking the lead. Ultor doesn't like it, but he doesn't hear them being called, and he can't move very fast, so he has to let her go ahead.

"Why is it that you have entered Asgard?" Odin directs the question to Jotur now since she seems to be the speaker of the group.

She answers, "We saw our parents taken by the Valkyries after a fierce battle with trolls, but they were still alive when they were taken, and we have come here to bring them home where they are needed."

Odin laughs out loud, astonished with the nerve of the children to think they can just walk into Asgard and take their parents home.

"You dare to question the gods?" Odin asks.

"Na-no, NO!" Jotur stutters a bit to find the right words, not wanting to offend him. "We just miss them so, and we were hoping it was a mistake."

"Those whom the Valkyrie choose to enter Valhalla become part of my army," Odin explains.

Feeling sorry for the little Vikings, Frigg puts her hand on her husband's arm, which rests on his chair, asking to speak. She addresses the children, "If they were taken whilst they live, then perhaps Brynhild deemed them worthy of entering Valhalla without facing the agony of death."

"But they weren't doing anything heroic. They were just sitting there!" Tredge burst out. The crowd giggles at his honesty. "...and we love them very much too, and that is why we are here to take them back!"

Yves jumps in front of Tredge, afraid he will anger Odin with his outburst. He realizes Odin is in an unusual position with all the on-lookers and that this is a sensitive situation. He doesn't want Odin to make an example out of them; though they have broken the law, his law, and punishment is inevitable. Yves speaks, trying to salvage the situation and save what life, if any, they still may have.

"I'm sorry for the intrusion. We're sorry. We didn't mean to break any laws or get Heimdall in trouble. We honestly didn't think we would make it this far. We went on this journey to find our parents because we didn't know what else to do and were overtaken with grief." Yves bows his head and doesn't make eye contact as a way to show respect. Odin stirs for a minute, looking as if he was taken by the boy's sorrow, but then speaks his judgment.

During the conversation between Yves and Odin, Jotur notices Loki has pushed his way past Odin's advisors and positioned himself next to Odin's side. She may not know the stories of the gods like Yves, but she does know Loki's reputation as the god of mischief and trickery. She has read that Loki has a strange influence on the other gods, and by using his cunning words, he can often convince them to do things they normally might not do.

"What's he up to?" Jotur whispers to Yves, who has no idea what she is talking about. Yves is focusing on Odin and pleading for their lives.

"Silence!" commands Odin. "No mortals who enter Asgard may leave; that is how it has always been. There will be no return for your parents, and the four of you will be sent to Nifilhel, where those unworthy of Valhalla must spend eternity." At Odin's harsh words, Loki, standing beside his father, begins to speak up. Tredge grabs Jotur's hand, and she reaches out and takes Yves'. The guards quickly surround the Vikings and begin to usher them back toward the entrance. Jotur is still watching the throne, looking for some shred of hope.

Loki's Cunningness

Loki has come up with an idea, a clever one he thinks, which will show Odin as a fair god and entertain the other gods and himself in the process. He has positioned himself to do so, and once Odin completes his sentencing, Loki respectfully leans in and begins his scheming.

"Surely, Great Odin, All-father, ruler of us all…," Loki whispers in his father's ear, knowing just how to cater to Odin's ego. "…these four mortals who have managed to find Bifrost, sneak past Heimdall the watcher, and enter Asgard's gate of their own accord are worthy of Valhalla." Loki looks up to see the children and Ultor being escorted out of the hall and continues knowing his time is short. "Perhaps even the elder would be a great asset to your army." He pauses to see if he has his father's attention. Odin nods, indicating he is listening, and Loki continues to explain.

"Why not challenge them to compete against Asgardians for the right to return home with their parents? If they win, they may take their parents home, but if they lose, they must enter Valhalla and serve you."

"Challenge the gods?" Odin asks Loki in disbelief. "That's insane; they will surely lose."

"Exactly, they will end up serving you here, and you will be seen as a fair and just leader." With that last statement, Loki leans back and lets him contemplate the proposition. Odin sits up straight on his throne, hesitating for a moment.

"Loki, you have a point," he tells him. "I like it!" Odin agrees to Loki's plan and clears his voice to address the audience.

"Stop!" he thunders as to get everyone's attention at one time.

Jotur, still watching Loki whisper into his father's ear, wonders what he was up to this time. '*This can't be good,*' she thinks, '*but anything is better than Nifilhel.*'

"Wait!" Odin tells the guards, holding his hand up. "Bring them here." The guards escorting the Vikings stop and redirect them back toward Odin. Confused, the children turn around and head back toward the throne, with Ultor lagging behind.

"I propose a contest," Odin announces to the crowd of onlookers. Odin thought he was being lenient with his first ruling by letting them not experience an agonizing death and enter Nifilhel, but Loki did have a good point. He will seem more just if it looks like the children have a chance to fight for their freedom and possibly their parents' freedom, even if the odds are against them.

The children, in disbelief, just stand there staring at him. The crowd chatters amongst themselves with questions of their own.

"Did he just challenge us?" Yves asks his sister.

"I think so, but what does that mean?" Jotur responds to her brother.

"No one ever challenges the gods, no human, that is," Yves says, wondering what kind of challenge they could possibly have a chance of winning against the gods.

"I don't know, but it's better than death. So, I'll take it!" Tredge says to them, not really understanding what Odin meant by a challenge, but he doesn't care.

"Do we have to accept?" Yves asks, knowing they don't have the answers.

"I have no idea," Jotur replies. "It's not like he asked us. It's more like he just announced it."

"Well, it's not like we have another choice," Yves replies.

Jotur, confused, steps forward. All eyes are on Odin now as if asking him to repeat himself. Everyone is watching, waiting for Odin's next words, for him to explain. Finally, Odin continues with his announcement.

"Vikings, I have decided we will have a competition for the lives of your parents and for your freedom." Odin looks down at the Vikings who stand before him, Tredge still in the middle. "You must win four challenges against the Asgardians to earn your parents' lives back and earn your own freedom. It is simple, one challenge for each of you and one for both of your parents. You may choose who does the fourth challenge for your parents." Tredge, Yves, and Jotur listen intensely to the rules.

He continues, "If you can defeat the Asgardians in four challenges, all five of you will go free, but if the Asgardians win just one of the events, you will have to choose who is set free and who will become my servants in Valhalla forever."

Tredge's mouth drops open. *'How will we ever choose who goes and who stays?'* he wonders.

Loki, still right by his father's side, leans in again and suggests, "Let the three children choose the competitions so that they may see how fair and just the noble Odin is." Of course, Odin does not care what the competitions are, for no Viking children can beat a god. But he thinks Loki is right; it might seem fairer if they can choose their own challenges, and it might just be more entertaining for the afternoon.

"As I am a just and fair god, I will allow you to choose the challenges," Odin says, agreeing with Loki. "…but each of you must perform at least one of the challenges," he adds. "And the events matter not, for these mere mortals will not defeat the Asgardians. Now, let Var, the goddess of oaths and promises, oversee this agreement and punish any who do not stand to its purpose and fulfillment."

Tredge leans over and looks up at Yves, "Do people grow old in Valhalla?"

"No," he says, annoyed at such a question with everything else going on.

Tredge mutters under his breath, "Great, I'm going to be nine and a half forever."

The trickster of the Norse gods knows precisely what he has suggested and is delighted at the idea of a day of mischief. He's gotten the Vikings out of Nifilhel and, at the same time, has given them a loophole, a very small one, but still a chance to fight for their freedom. Loki knows they won't win, but now at least the children will have the opportunity to stay in Valhalla, where he knows their parents are located.

Judgment of Ultor

Odin turns his attention to Ultor, having almost forgotten about him. "And you, old man?" he asks, though Ultor doesn't really know what he is asking. "Do you think I have forgotten what you have done?" he asks again, with Ultor unable to answer. "It has been settled as to why the children came to Asgard, but what about you? You should know better than to pierce the gates of Asgard. So, why do you accompany children to Asgard? To help them?"

Ultor steps forward and explains, "Honestly, I didn't think the children would ever find Bifrost. I was hoping to find them a new home. They were alone and had no one but each other and couldn't have survived the winter. I thought a neighboring village might take them in. I wanted to find a home for them, being the only elder left in town…and if I died in the process, perhaps it would seem noble enough for Valhalla."

Ultor humbly bows and continues, "I have fought, defended, and protected my people for many years in the name of Thor, Thunder god, who sits yonder." He points toward Thor. "I was never slain in battle because I fought bravely and won, but now suffer from old age. I wish not to die thusly, so I come hither to enter Valhalla myself to serve you, O Mighty Odin, in your army."

"Think you, Ultor, that I know not of your deeds in battle? Tales of your success and prowess have often reached my ears by my ravens. Your trust in those children has brought you hither, now, so that is where your fate must lie." Odin pauses and signals for Var.

"Correction," he tells her. "The children will compete in five challenges. They will also fight for the freedom of Ultor, their elder." Odin turns to Ultor and addresses him once more. "You shall share in their fate but not in their competitions. Your judgment shall depend on their outcome, for they will fight for your life too. Var is witness to this addendum and will ensure its fairness. Now let the children choose their first competition." Upon Odin raising the challenges to five, the children look over at Ultor, who seems crushed he can't join the fight and help them. Jotur bows her head, hiding her face and the look of despair, heavy with the thought of one more life in their hands.

CHAPTER IV

THE CHALLENGES
· · · · · · · · · · · · · · ·

The children are escorted to the entrance of The Arena of Fate by the guards and are left there to walk through the front gate alone. Ultor is not permitted to accompany them even into the arena. Tredge, looking all around, takes in every sight, smell, and sound to memory. It is a large marble stone arena with immense columns and stadium-style seating in a semi-circle horseshoe shape around an open field for battle. A canapé with a chair fit for a king is amidst the center of them. Tredge, Jotur, and Yves enter feeling small and insignificant below the large scaled structure. It has all the grandeur you deem fit for Asgard's gods. Upon reaching the center, they stand, motionless, in the middle of the Asgardian arena in awe.

News of these three young Vikings who are taking on the mighty gods travels fast in the kingdom, and the arena begins to fill up.

Jotur speaks up first.

"I can't believe this! Challenging the gods? It was all Loki's idea. I saw him plotting!" she says, angry over his meddling.

"Well, if it weren't for him, we would be in Niflhel right now," Tredge tells her, sticking up for his favorite god Loki.

"We have to plan out and plot our every move and evaluate every possible outcome before we make any decisions," Yves tells them. Distracted, Tredge is looking around at the gathering crowd, already not paying attention to his brother, or so Yves thinks.

"Tredge, listen!" Yves tugs at his shirt to get his attention. "All eyes must be open walking into each challenge,"

"Hey! I listen with my ears!" he tells his brother. "Plus, my teachers were boring in school, so I studied the gods a lot," he admits, turning his wide eyes toward Yves to give him his full attention.

"Yeah, that will help. We must draw from every ounce of our knowledge of the gods, their powers, history...anything we can think of, if there's any chance of us winning," Yves says, looking at Tredge specifically.

"Okay, so one challenge at a time," Jotur reminds them. "We know these gods and their strengths and weaknesses. We just have to think."

"Weaknesses? They're gods!" Tredge states. "They don't have weaknesses."

"You know what she means. We can pool our knowledge together. We have skills too, you know. We have to be clever," Yves says. "...And we can challenge

Asgardians, who are not necessarily gods," Yves reminds them, already thinking of a challenge.

"Yeah, one challenge is impossible, but five is crazy!" Jotur starts to tear up. "Why five if they think they are so unbeatable?"

"I don't know; perhaps we are the day's entertainment," Yves says as he looks up and sees the crowds still gathering, then shakes his head, trying not to get distracted. "Stay positive. We just need to focus and take one challenge at a time."

"Yeah, if we fight well enough, at least we can stay in Valhalla and make Ultor happy," Tredge tells them as he finds Ultor in the audience, sitting front and center. "That's thinking positive!"

"Okay, that's not quite the positive I was looking for," Yves tells Tredge. "I have an idea, though."

"We…we have an idea," Tredge corrects him.

Jotur is eager to hear what the two have in mind for the first challenge. She knows they must have something clever brewing between them. She had seen the two whispering, as her brothers do, discussing something when leaving the Hall, but was too afraid to ask.

Yves begins to explain the first competition to her. "An ice sculpting contest with the dwarfs, Brokk and Eitri."

"What? Are you crazy? I've seen their talents!" Jotur exclaims.

"But I can do it! I'm good too!" Tredge defends himself.

"Shhhh, think it through," Yves hushes him, not wanting to give their challenge away until they are ready.

Jotur isn't so sure of their idea. "Yes, you are good, Tredge, but they are master carvers!"

"But I've studied their work," Tredge reports. "They are magnificent but not perfect."

"Not perfect?" Jotur asks, not understanding what the boys are referring to.

"They messed up on Thor's hammer," Yves reminds her. "Didn't you read that?"

"Aaghhh, true, yes," Jotur concurs. "Okay, so the handle was too short. It isn't perfect, but their work is still amazing."

Yves speaks up, "and so is Tredge. He may be young, but they will underestimate him."

"Okay, but you have to be sharp if we are to win," Jotur says, agreeing to their first challenge. "Plus, if you think about it, the dwarfs will be of their element. Make sure the challenge takes place in the arena."

"Yeah, out of their cave to compete, and they won't like that. And it will be under the conditions of the challenge, not theirs; they won't like that either. Dwarfs are very obstinate!" Yves agrees the different environment might throw them off their game.

"Okay, all agree?" Yves asks, leaning toward them in a huddle so as not to allow the gods to hear their plan. Silly thought on his part, he realizes. The gods are arrogant and probably believe a strategy won't even be helpful for the little Vikings. They whisper nonetheless. They do not want anyone to report to Odin how clever they really are, or so they think.

As the Asgardians are gathering in the arena, they pay no attention to the children huddled in the center discussing their plans. Once the three young Vikings have decided on their challenge, they wait patiently on Odin's arrival.

'*There's a chance,*' Jotur tells herself, '*...slim, but still a chance.*'

"Remember that the gods think they are unbeatable, unbreakable, and indestructible, and that is their weakness," she reminds the boys.

"What is opportunity?" Tredge asks heartily. It is a familiar question their father would ask every year before the festival. The children would always answer in unison, "*99% preparation and 1% perspiration!*"

"Oh, and what about '*You have been preparing for this challenge all your lives,*?'" Yves adds, quoting their father. "Yeah, I wonder what Dad would say now."

"He would probably give us the clan speech. The one that goes, '*It is our time to represent the ones who have stepped before us, for without their footprints, we would not exist!*'" Yves says, deepening his voice to sound more like their father.

"Or, '*It is with their strength and courage we stand here today!*'" Jotur adds.

"Very well said, sis," Yves smiles, pleased with her contribution.

"Hey, we are in Asgard, and I haven't seen them yet. Why aren't Mom and Dad here?" Tredge asks. Jotur and Yves ignore the questions but are wondering the same thing.

"Are you guys ready?!" Yves asks, seeing Odin enter the arena.

Yves takes out his sword and lifts it up. Tredge and Jotur take out their weapons and do the same, making a clanging sound as they bring them together. Some in the crowd look for the sound, and others pay no attention. With the noise, however, Odin does take notice.

"Are you ready?" Odin speaks out, and the crowd hushes. Jotur steps forward.

"We have our first challenge," Jotur says.

"Well, do tell," Odin says, intrigued, believing the little Viking children are naive and speak too quickly without thinking things all the way through.

Challenge 1: Ignorance is not Bliss

After hearing Jotur explain the challenge, Odin quickly summons the dwarfs, Brokk and Eitri, and a large stealthy-looking being enters the arena. The children watch him take his steps with dirt swirling behind his heels as he kicks the dry dust up from the ground.

"Who is that?" Tredge asks.

"I have no idea," Yves answers. "I don't think it's Brokk or Eitri."

The creature drags his feet ever so slowly, walking toward the center of the arena. The crowd ignores his entrance and continues chattering amongst themselves. He is hunched over, human-like, with his head cocked to the left side as if it is stuck. As odd as he seems, the air about him is gentle. As he walks through the arena, Tredge, Yves, and Jotur can't keep their eyes off of him, though he has made no effort to look at the Viking children. Apparently, he doesn't even warrant an introduction, a lowly place in the social structure of the gods. In his hands, he carries two wooden tackle boxes.

Tredge studies him as he approaches, wondering to himself, *'Shouldn't the tackle boxes balance him? And if so, why is he leaning to the right?'* Tredge keeps his question to himself for once and keeps his eyes on the boxes, wondering their purpose.

Jotur breaks the stares of the three and finally turns to the boys and speaks, "He looks like a farrier coming to shoe a horse," she whispers.

"Make that two horses," Yves responds, keeping watch over the stranger. But there are no horses in the arena. No shoes to clip or repair.

"What are the tools for?" Tredge asks. They are all wondering the same thing, scared of the answer.

As Tredge watches the creature walk slowly across the arena, he wonders, *'Where does this person or being come from? And how come no one else seems alarmed at his strange look or slinky gate of a walk? Do they all know him and his story, or do they even care? 'NO!'* he tells himself, *'I need to remain focused, no wondering questions,'* and he turns his attention back to the tackle boxes, focusing in on them. Upon looking closer, he realizes the tools are for sculpting, not horses.

"Oh no, I need tools too!" Tredge says, grabbing Yves' arm. "We didn't think about asking for tools. I need *tools. I didn't think about tools!*" His heart races. He's starting to think this is a challenge already lost. His siblings notice the doubts surfacing in him and the panic on his face.

"You do this all the time at home, sculpt that is," Yves says to him.

"But tools, I need tools too!" Tredge says, pointing at the toolboxes being carried by the creature.

"...And he has two sets. I bet one is yours," Jotur tells him to calm him down, not sure herself if the tools are for him.

"A challenge among gods, with gods, we must be crazy. What were we thinking?" Tredge asks his siblings, not expecting an answer, for he is merely rambling his anxieties out loud.

"They're dwarfs, not gods," she reminds him. "Don't worry; you got this!" Jotur says to encourage him, though secretly needing some inspiration herself.

"Don't doubt your talent," Yves demands. "...and just focus on yourself, not them."

"Yeah, you focus on what you have to do, your task, not theirs," Jotur says, always mothering him. "Don't even look over at them."

"Speaking of them, where are they?" Tredge asks.

"*BOOOM!*" A loud noise rings out across the arena. The three Vikings jump with alarm in unison. Without leaning down, the creature drops both tackle boxes, startling them and awakening the crowd. The gods quickly turn their attention to the center of the arena as though the dropping of the tackle boxes is telling them it is time to begin. The awkward stranger proceeds to leave the arena with the same sluggish gate with which he entered. Within seconds the dwarfs appear across from Tredge with the boxes lying directly between them. Tredge tries to look closer at the contents without taking a step. In fear of breaking a rule or making the gods angry, he examines them only with his eyes. He doesn't walk over to them and stoop down to look as the dwarfs do, and he doesn't touch them either. Definitely no touching. He doesn't know if he can approach them yet, but he can tell that the toolboxes are identical with carving tools carefully organized. When he finally does look at the box, he examines its contents as carefully as possible. He recognizes the tools and reads them off in his mind very quickly.

'One long carving knife, one mallet, two stakes, a hook knife, mounted stones, and two chisels on the right side placed within those small brown nooks…a small hammer, bloom forge clip, larger hammer in the left side pocket.' He doesn't want to waste time searching for items and quickly tries to memorize each piece of equipment and its location.

"Are you ready?" Odin asks though Tredge wonders if he is talking to him, the dwarfs, or both. He doesn't answer but nods just in case it is him. The dwarfs look up at Odin as if to agree to start, and the noise of thunder begins to roll in the clouds. The noise gets closer and eventually is directly over the arena. Then, as suddenly as a bolt of lightning, a frost giant from the land of Niflhel, a land of ice with nine frozen rivers, appears before them. The giant provides two solid blocks of ice and places them in the middle of the arena for all to see.

Odin begins to speak, "Both these slabs of raw material come from the purest body of water, formed in a range of temperatures from the frigged airs of the north to the most resilient lands of ice of the gods," Odin explains to the audience as he points toward the blocks of thick ice proudly.

"Yeah!" Fenrir, the son of Loki, is watching close by and speaks out like an impatient child with excitement. "These blocks are made for sculpting and are free from imperfections." Odin's grandson's interruption annoys him. Odin doesn't like interruptions or disrespect in front of guests and the gods. Odin looks at Fenrir with irritation, clears his voice to make the disapproval known, and continues to speak.

"Though their time is limited, it is entirely up to the sculptors to bring the ice blocks to life." Odin gestures to the dwarfs, ignoring Tredge. The dwarfs are well known for their creativity and details when it comes to sculpting, especially Brokk and Eitri. Unbeknownst to the children, Brokk and Eitri do all the sculptures for the galleries and celebrations in Asgard. In fact, the gods have the dwarfs sculpt whatever or whoever they want at every occasion in Asgard. Their portfolio ranges from carvings of various gods and goddesses, realms such as Alfheim, the land of the elves, to even Odin's two ravens, Huginn and Muninn. The list is long of their many accomplishments in Asgard, but no one has ever actually seen them work.

"It will be a great pleasure for the gods to see Brokk and Eitri do their magic," Odin says to the crowd, pleased with the two dwarfs the children have chosen to compete against in their first challenge.

"You may pick up your tools and begin," Odin says, starting the competition.

***

Tredge doesn't spend as much time thinking about the *'what'* to carve as he does on the *'how.'* He knows exactly what to carve, and he also knows Asgard is not a very cold environment, and he must work quickly if he wants to finish his piece in time. At home, he could make a snowman like no other from ice, and it would stay around all winter, but it only took one semi-warm day in the spring for his art piece to begin to melt, lost forever. With this in mind, he begins to work without hesitation.

As the small Viking and even smaller dwarfs are given the go-ahead to begin their diligent work on their ice sculptures, the crowd falls quiet, turning their attention to the dwarfs. With the gods' and goddesses' attention on the competition at hand, Tredge feels the pressure of their eyes upon him, staring him down and burning the back of his head. But this is all in his head, he tells himself, pushing back his feelings and starting to work. Unbeknownst to him, he is right, for they aren't watching him anyway, but rather Brokk and Eitri.

Tredge begins to work diligently on his piece and quickly tunes out those around him. He focuses deep in thought as if he is the only one in the arena. Tredge first stoops down and squats simultaneously, as only a child can do, and still stay on their feet. Then he stands straight up, turns, and walks over to the left side of the block, measuring with his eyes three and a half feet up the block. He is now ready to begin. He grabs a big blunt hammer and a stake out of the tackle box, and with one big swing, the first strike of the competition is made by him.

Egil, who is standing next to Odin, grumbles, "Aachum!" trying to get the dwarfs' attention. He is one of Odin's servants and married to a Valkyrie. His attempts to prompt the dwarfs to start sculpting come to no avail. Brokk and Eitri both ignore the gesture and remain whispering among themselves. The conversation is intense, and neither of them breaks away from the other. It is obviously a serious dispute of creative differences. The audience soon bores with their lack of work, and attention begins to waver. Before long, the crowd begins to chatter amongst themselves.

This is actually the first time Brokk and Eitri have ever been outside of the mining caves, outside of their elements, and placed on display. The two are not used to people, gods, or life outside their homes. They usually work without an audience and alone. Discussions before the first cut might be a norm for them. No one knows how they usually work together or how they create their masterpieces.

Meanwhile, as Brokk and Eitri seem to be discussing the block of ice, Tredge continues to work diligently. He continues to pay no attention to the distractions coming from the gods' constant chatter. But, from the corner of his eye, he can see the dwarfs standing by their block of ice. As far as he can tell, the dwarfs are still debating over the sculpture design or where to start, and they have barely made a chip in it.

'You can't get distracted by them,' he tells himself. He glances slightly in the opposite direction toward his

brother and sister, where he gets two thumbs-up from Yves and an encouraging smile from Jotur.

A few minutes pass, and even Odin is getting annoyed with the little dwarfs. It is beginning to border on a lack of respect in Odin's book that they still haven't begun. Egil takes his cue once again and tries, louder this time, to get their attention, encouraging them to start. "Aaa-chummm!" he coughs, and the crowd, hearing this loud gesture, looks up from their engaging conversations with neighbors and friends. Obviously, the king's assistant is not clearing his throat this time but trying to get the dwarfs' attention before the king loses his patience. Odin is already displeased with the delay, and everyone can see it.

Tredge continues to remind himself to remain focused. "Blinders, blinders," he mumbles, reminding himself he must focus on his work and have blinders on shielding him from all the possible distractions.

"Brokk and Eitri," Egil finally speaks up, though quietly, to get their attention. When he calls out the dwarfs' names, Brokk and Eitri turn and look at him, annoyed with the interruption. They are never interrupted when working alone in their cave workshop.

"The competition has begun," Egil says to them kindly so as not to make them mad, adding a slight smile.

The two, not so quickly, scuffle to their little feet to gather their tools, bringing them closer to the ice block. Brokk walks over to the sculpting tools provided by the hunchback, dirt-shuffling blacksmith's assistant, and peers into the box as if it has cooties. Brokk then picks up a hook knife from the box with just two fingers as if to touch it as minimally as possible. He inspects it and holds it up for Eitri to examine too, who condescendingly snarls up his nose. Eitri counters with a chisel, and Brokk shakes his head against it. The two have another discussion, though the crowd can only imagine it is about the rest of the tools in the set. It is obvious they are not good enough for the master sculptors, especially after the two are seen walking away from the toolbox empty-handed. They quickly send for their own tools. King Odin is not pleased with the delay or their self-centeredness, but as soon as their tools are received from their underground forge, they turn back to the block of ice to make their first strike.

As the crowd becomes restless watching the dwarfs begin their work at what seems to be a long-drawn-out ritual of theirs, they quickly turn their attention to Tredge, who is fast at work. The crowd forgets the chaos of Brokk and Eitri, falling silent as their curiosity begins to peak. Tredge's sculpture is beginning to take shape. He works attentively, chipping away at the ice with the tools of the unknown creature. He works fast, not knowing if there is a time limit or if time is called whenever someone finishes. He doesn't ask; he doesn't speak; he just works as fast and clean as he can. Even Odin looks up from his group of advisors, noticing the crowds' silence, and is amazed at the mere mortal. No one mutters a word. Until half past noontime, only an hour into the competition, Tredge stands back, leans in to make a few simple corrections with his chisel and file, and then says, "I'm finished."

Yves, sitting on the sand and gravel ground of the arena, nudges his sister, who is sitting right next to him. She is staring off, looking toward the distant landscape of the walls of people, gods, and servants, searching for something.

"Jotur," he says, trying to get her attention as he apparently interrupts her train of thought. Her eyes immediately jump to Tredge, and she leaps to her feet. Both start to head toward Tredge without thinking if it is even allowed or what is next. As she is about to reach Tredge, she stops, reaching her hand out to grab Yves' and gives it a squeeze. Yves doesn't look at her or his hand but stares at the very sight she is seeing.

There, standing before them, is a wonderous sculpture made of pure water and ice yet elegant with its simplicity. The simple marks and shavings made from his chisel came together to form a grand gesture. Seeing their expressions, Tredge responds.

"Pretty good, huh?" he asks, proud of his sculpture. Tredge stands there admiring his work. At his feet are tiny morsels of shaved ice that quickly fade into the gravel of rock and sandstone. Larger pieces are melting at a slower pace, but nonetheless, melting, softening, then liquefying into the peat-gravel below. Tredge's feet stand among the shavings, his boots wet from thawing chips and his hands slightly numb from the constant contact with the ice.

"It's Brynhild!" someone in the crowd shouts. Now all the eyes are upon the sculpture if they weren't before. The gods are amazed at the young Vikings' ice statue.

"It *is* Brynhild," Jotur says to Yves in amazement.

"The majestic leader of the Valkyries," he replies. Jotur and Yves do not take their eyes off it, taking in every detail. Tredge has carved Brynhild riding upon a winged steed with her sword held high. In school, Tredge would study the ancient records and accounts of history that some villagers believed to be true and others to be pure myth. He studied them for his wood carvings, memorizing the pictures, each god, their realm, and power, and Brynhild was one of his favorites. He knew every crease of her hand as it reached up toward the sky holding the mighty sword, her face as night's light fell upon it. He knew the softness of the horse's wings which had to be illuminated.

"Look! It's me. He sculpted me!" she says in delight. Brynhild begins to praise his work and offers her approval in the hoarfrost statuette with applause as she begins to rise. The crowd, seeing her reaction to Tredge's ice sculpture, starts to cheer in delight along with her. Tredge smiles in satisfaction at her approval. Yves and Jotur smile proudly at their brother. Now the three Vikings stand together, leaning into each other.

"There is no way a dwarf, let alone two, can beat this ovation," Yves says to Tredge. At that time, Tredge realizes he hasn't even seen the dwarfs' sculpture yet. He can't see it for the immensity of his own masterpiece.

"What about the dwarfs?" Yves asks, realizing they had been so focused on Tredge's sculpture that they didn't even look to see what his opponents were sculpting.

"I'm not sure, are they done?" Jotur asks.

Tredge looks over at his siblings. Yves and Jotur share a slight look of panic.

Jotur takes Tredge's hand. "It can't be any better," she says, reaffirming him and herself.

"The gods haven't said anything, and I can't see it," Yves replies. Tredge's sculpture is between them and the dwarfs. Tredge takes the first step, and the other two follow toward the opponents. He walks around his sculpture to take a peek when he suddenly stops in his tracks. The other two almost bump into him. But, then, all they hear is Odin's authoritative voice, speaking out to the crowd.

"Wait!" Odin says, disgruntled. He sits up. "The challenge isn't over yet," he says as he quiets the crowd with one raise of his hand. He continues, "That sculpture may be nice, but let's see what the magnificent Brokk and Eitri have brought forth from the ice."

As Tredge takes another step around his sculpture, he can just imagine magical gods dancing, grand musical instruments, or fighting Asgardians in a victorious battle. Then as his eyes meet Brokk and Eitri, he gasps, and his mouth falls open in astonishment. Jotur and Yves look quickly, hearing his surprise, and react with the same utterance to the sight, as does every Asgardian and on-looker present. Even Odin gasps. It is as if everyone sees the dwarfs' work at the same time.

There, before the dwarfs, hammers in their hands, belts around their waists, holding dry tools, there is nothing. Nothing but soot, nothing but dirt and water, turned to mud. Brokk and Eitri look down, their feet in the middle of a puddle, as they can see their reflection on the ground. The soot from their clothes, the heat from using their own tools, and the warmth of hands from years in the forges have melted the block of ice. They didn't have a sculpture. They didn't have any ice. It has all melted by their doing. They are ashamed as they bow their heads low, their eyes seeming to plead forgiveness and pity from the gods. Odin waves his hand again, this time motioning for the dwarfs to be escorted out of the arena. Tredge hopes they aren't in too much trouble, but he doesn't ask where they are being taken or if they are being punished. He is learning to keep his mouth shut, especially around the gods.

In a matter of seconds, the dwarfs are out of sight and gone from the arena. It finally hits Tredge, *'I've won! I beat the dwarfs!'*

"Outwitted dwarfs?" Jotur says as if she is reading his mind. She walks up and stands by Tredge's side, putting her arm around him. "Little brother, you play well with dwarfs!" she teases.

'She was right all along,' Tredge thinks to himself, but he isn't going to tell her that. Yves joins them and quietly speaks where only they can hear.

"Very clever, Yves. Challenging the dwarfs…," she tells him. "…but now what?"

"Four more challenges," he answers. The children gather together, facing each other in a huddle to keep others from hearing their words.

"One at a time," Jotur reminds them. "Just take one challenge at a time." With the first competition complete, they realize more than ever how they must think before they act, especially if they want to continue to outwit the Asgardians. Luckily, during all of Tredge's hard work, his brother and sister have already been planning the next challenge. With a look of support from Jotur, Yves steps forward to face Odin.

Challenge 2: Let Go My Ego

Yves speaks up. "I will take on the next challenge." And he steps forward.

"Yes, let's move things along." Odin is ready to forget the dwarfs. He never actually admits outright defeat of Brokk and Eitri, but it isn't necessary. Knowing he needs to choose his words wisely, Yves steps forward and clearly to address Odin and the audience.

"I would like to challenge the thunder god, Thor," he announces. The onlookers immediately turn their attention to Yves. He can see the expressions of shock in everyone's face with the sheer mention of Thor's name.

"Thor?" Odin asks. The mere mention of challenging Thor almost has Odin leaping out of his chair with intrigue. He puts his hands on each side of his throne and sits straight up. Everyone can see that Odin is excited by the children's choice.

Yves continues, "I want to challenge him to a race through the North Seas, which we crossed to get here." Thor is often associated with thunder, lightning, and storms, so the frigid air of the North Sea shouldn't be problematic for him.

Odin smiles again. "The NORTH Sea?" he asks for clarity, thinking the small childish Viking has made a mistake. The North Sea is bitter cold, with rigid temperatures and rough waters. "Why would a young boy even try to race Thor, let alone in a climate so difficult for a mere mortal?" Odin asks rhetorically.

Tredge, not knowing what is going on, glances at his sister and quietly asks, "What is Yves thinking?" She shushes him, so he whispers so as not to be heard by others and asks again, "Jotur, what are you thinking? Yves can't race a god let alone Thor! He is not just any god, but a major god! A hammer wielding fighting machine god!"

"Trust us," is all Jotur replies, keeping her attention on Yves, not even making eye contact with Tredge. She may have doubts of her own about Yves' idea to challenge Thor, but she isn't going to show it.

"Silence!" Odin shouts. He is pleased with the idea of Thor in a challenge and knows the children will not be able to win against such a warrior. As soon as the name "*Thor*" is out of Yves' mouth, Odin is ready to seal the deal.

Tredge quickly gathers next to his sister's side. He doesn't like the shouting. He grabs her hand, which used to have a calming effect on his fears, but they aren't in Svalbard anymore, and, to his dismay, it isn't helping. A simple sisterly presence to wipe away the worries doesn't seem to be enough anymore. His previous life is a mere blur in his memory, life before the discovery of trolls, Valkyries, and Bifrost. Tredge remains silent hoping they have a plan, hoping Yves and Jotur have thought this all through to the end.

"It is settled then. Thor will be the second challenger," Odin says with pride. The crowd cheers. Everyone knows Odin is proud of his son Thor and that he will represent the gods and all of Asgard well.

"Let it be so," says Odin, clapping three times to call upon Thor. He is summoned from his realm, Trondheim, and before they can blink, he appears before them. The mighty god is adorned with a helmet, iron gloves, a hammer, and a belt to increase his great strength. The Vikings can't believe it. Thor now stands by his father's side right in front of Yves, Tredge, and Jotur.

"Son, would you kindly race this boy today?" his father asks.

"But he is a mere mortal," Thor replies. "It doesn't seem quite fair."

"It may not be fair, but you are their choice," Odin explains. His father quickly explains about the Valkyries taking their parents, the Vikings trespassing into Asgard, and the fight for their freedom. Thor is impressed with the little Vikings.

"I will race, for you father, if it is your will," and with that, Thor bows at his father's feet, accepting the challenge. Thor turns and smiles at the little Vikings, then begins to walk down into the arena to join Yves. All the while laughter and cheering can be heard amidst the crowd.

"There is no turning back now," Jotur says to Tredge, still holding her hand.

Without any notice, Thor and Yves are transported to the beautiful shoreline of Greenland. Yves finds himself once again standing on the outermost point of the North Sea shore, where the bitter cold takes his breath away. Yet, he feels a sense of comfort, having been there before. The cold doesn't seem to faze Thor, who stands tall and muscular, and isn't at all bothered by the sudden climate change. Yves knows he will not go easy on him, and Thor will be eager to show off his speed and parade his skill, for he is a god. Yves notices he has his mighty hammer in hand, and smiles. It is as Yves had predicted. He also notices Thor is adorned with his belt as he had hoped, as well as his iron gauntlets, which Yves had not expected. Yves tries to keep his smile hidden from his opponent. The gauntlets will play perfectly into his plans.

"The two of you, Thor and the Viking Yves, are to race across the North Sea and whoever reaches the other side first is the winner," Odin clarifies. "The burst of thunder will be the sign to begin the race."

The gods and spectators from Asgard view the race by peering through the clouds as if looking through a large magnifying glass. Word has traveled across Asgard, and every creature, god, and goddess gather to see the brave children who challenge the gods and the boy who dares to race Thor. Thor, son of Odin, the god coupled with strength, a god you want to be alongside, not against.

Tredge and Jotur watch as Yves takes his place just as intensely as if they were right there on the coast with him. As Yves stands on the shore waiting for the signal to start he closes his eyes and listens to the quiet sounds of the arctic. The seconds leading up to the thunder seem like hours. He can hear his heart beating, feeling it begin to race in his chest. He takes a deep breath and counts to ten as his dad taught him to do before every competition at the festival.

Suddenly, Yves hears a *KABOOM!* and jumps, startled by the sound. The race has begun. Thor, hearing the thunder, without hesitating, takes a few steps and leaps into the water. Still wearing his usual attire, Thor instantly sinks to the bottom. It seems he plans to run across the bottom of the sea and reach the other side before Yves can even step foot in the water. But Yves hasn't moved yet. He doesn't run toward the shoreline nor jump in the water as everyone expects.

Tredge, impatiently cries out, "Run, Yves!" not realizing he probably can't hear him. *'Why is he not running?'* he thinks to himself.

"Wait for it," Jotur says quietly to Tredge. "Just wait for it."

"So he does have a plan!" Tredge whispers. *'But of course, Yves has a plan; he always has a plan. I shouldn't have doubted him,'* Tredge thinks now. He knows Yves would not have chosen Thor without some kind of strategy.

Thor is well on his way just a few short minutes after the thunderous noise crossing the North Sea. But Yves, on the other hand, is still on the shore. He begins to walk calmly over to the water's edge. When he gets there, he slaps the surface three times. His actions are very precise. He hits the water three times with his hand, no more, no less. Everyone watches intensely with curiosity. In the distance the surface of the water breaks. A few seconds later, it breaks again but closer to the shore, and then again even closer. The interruptions on the surface of the water become more frequent in a sort of pattern. The interludes between each shorten and the breaks come closer. Everyone's attention is turned toward the sea in anticipation. As the breaks get closer a figure can finally be seen and suddenly water shoots high up into the air.

The onlookers gasp in delight.

"Look!" Tredge yells excitedly, "Look, it is Brodnak!"

Brodnak surfaces as he reaches the shoreline. Odin watches as Yves approaches the giant whale, sure he will be eaten. Astonishment fills the arena at the bravery and lack of fear demonstrated by the Viking. With everyone's eyes upon him, Yves bends down and whispers in Brodnak's ear. Brodnak stays motionless, listening to the little Viking. Yves quickly explains how their journey did indeed lead them to Asgard.

"Brodnak, with your help crossing the sea, we reached the bridge leading into Asgard, which we stealthily crossed!"

"You crossed Bifrost and are still alive?" Brodnak asks, surprised.

"For now," Yves replies, giving Brodnak a pat on his side and laughing.

"So the stories are true," he responds in awe.

"Yes, Asgard, the bridge, the gods, oh and the gods, yes, the gods...," Yves continues to tell him about their current predicament.

"Boy, you get yourself in some jams, don't you?" Brodnak laughs. "I can't wait to hear what you are planning next."

Yves shakes his head, "One challenge at a time Brodnak. Now, I think we can win this one with your help."

All this time the gods are watching, analyzing their every move, wondering what they could possibly be talking about. They aren't listening in, of course, for that would be rude and discourteous, but they are watching. Spellbound, they can't believe this weak mortal is talking to a great whale, and not just any whale but the mighty Brodnak, without fear. Brodnak and Yves don't even realize they have an audience.

"My help, what can I do?" Brodnak asks, wondering what Yves has in mind.

"Swim!" Yves answers.

"Well, I can do that for sure!" Brodnak agrees. "You helped me, I'll help you!" Yves is relieved Brodnak is on board because he doesn't have a backup plan.

"Great!" Yves says, "But we kind of need to hurry; we're in a race...right now."

"Okay, let's get going then!" Brodnak agrees. He moves closer to the shore as Yves walks out into the shallow waters to meet him. Yves turns before he mounts the great whale and climbs up on Brodnak's back. With Yves holding on tightly, Brodnak takes off swiftly.

"So, who are we racing?"

"Thor," Yves answers nonchalantly.

"WHO?" Brodnak asks having heard him but needing to hear it again in disbelief?

"Thor, you know, protector of mankind, god of thunder, Thor?!" Yves explains like Brodnak doesn't know who Thor is.

"Okay, yeah, I know who Thor is, the one with the big hammer, right?" Brodnak replies playfully.

"Mjölnir," Yves confirms.

"What?" Brodnak asks Yves, confused by his answer.

"Mjölnir is the name of Thor's hammer," Yves tells him.

"Oh, I didn't know that. Why challenge Thor?" he asks.

"Just a hunch," Yves tells Brodnak.

"A hunch?" Brodnak says, deciding to let it go in the hopes that Yves knows what he is doing. Yves is one of the first humans the whale knows personally, and he decides he doesn't understand his logic very well.

"Trust me?" Yves replies.

"It is your life, or should I say, yours, your sister's, your brother's, and that old fellow's, but not mine, right?" Brodnak confirms just in case.

"No, you are right, just ours," Yves smiles as he reassures him.

Meanwhile, Thor continues to run on the floor of the sea. No one has seen him since he left the shore. The Viking can't swim in the North Sea due to the frigid waters and he assumes the mortal is taking a boat. Thor knows he is faster than any boat and thinks he has plenty of time, so he doesn't run his fastest but rather enjoys the scenery of the bottom of the sea. He has no idea what has transpired on the surface.

***

The sapphire colored waters spray up and shower Yves' face as he intensely watches up ahead for any sign of Thor.

"You okay up there?" Brodnak asks as he speeds across the top of the surface of the water. He is trying to keep an eye on Yves, knowing the icy waters can be dangerous to humans if they are overexposed. The cold doesn't seem to be bothering Yves though, adrenalin is racing through his veins as he tries to hang on to Brodnak.

"Yeah," Yves answers, "I'm doing just fine!" he yells back over the waves of rushing water. He is holding on to Brodnak's blowhole as there seems to be no other place to hold on and, despite the cold, he is actually enjoying the ride. "If Mom and Dad could see me now!" he yells joyfully. He can't believe he is actually riding a whale.

Only twenty minutes into the race, there is no sign of the shore or Thor. Brodnak swerves right and Yves holds on tight. As Yves looks closer at the water, it seems as if the waves have eyes. He thinks his eyes must be getting tired or have sea salt in them, but Brodnak laughs out loud.

"What? What is that?" he asks.

"Look!" Brodnak tells him. "Look real close!"

It is just as Yves thought; there are eyes looking at him from the waves. And just as Brodnak laughs boastfully a dolphin comes up from the waters below and splashes Yves and Brodnak. Two more dolphins jump out of the wake and do summersaults showing off their acrobatics, then disappear in the white foam to the sea below. Tredge laughs and others from the crowd follow, breaking the tension of the race.

"How many are there?" Tredge asks Jotur. "Can you tell?"

"More than one and less than four," she responds in her usual sarcastic manner.

And just as quickly as they appeared, the dolphins retire back into the ocean. Brodnak has victoriously crossed Yves over the finish line. Yves was so busy watching the dolphins he doesn't even notice. However, Thor is nowhere in sight.

Tredge and Jotur jump up and down with excitement not noticing if anyone is watching them celebrate. But suddenly, Tredge looks and Odin isn't at his throne anymore. He hopes his wrath isn't placed on them.

Thor, not knowing what has just happened, is immediately plucked from the bottom of the North Sea. Var, the goddess of oaths and promises, has transported him back to Asgard. Back to the side of his father's seat, which is now empty. Yves, however, is still talking to Brodnak.

"I can't thank you enough Brodnak, you are very fast!" Yves tells his friend and gives him a pat as he slides off his back.

"Well of course, I'm a whale!" Brodnak is shocked Yves would think otherwise. "Call again if you ever need me. It was fun. And good luck with the gods!"

Once Yves is completely out of the water, he, too, is transported back to Asgard. When he arrives Tredge and Jotur run to greet him.

"Two challenges, two victories, and three to go," Jotur whispers in his ear as she hugs him tightly.

He smiles brightly at his brother and sister, then looks around. "Where is Odin?" Yves asks.

"We have no idea, we were watching you race and didn't see him leave," Jotur explains.

King Odin is busy eating lunch when the race is completed and does not see who crossed over the finish line first, or at all. He had been hungry and taken a break from the day's excitements to eat undisturbed. He felt as long as his son Thor was racing a mortal, there was no need to watch. He has already decided where and how the Vikings are going to serve him in Asgard. However, when the news reaches Odin of the victor, there is a loud roar of thunder that rocks Asgard and he appears back in the arena immediately.

"So, what do you have to say for yourself?" Odin asks as Thor stands next to him, still confused.

"I ran my race," he replies, taking a knee and bowing his head to his father.

"Did you?" Odin asks. "Perhaps your tendency of acting first and thinking later may have played a role here. Did you see your opponent start the race?" Thor did not answer. He realizes he didn't actually see Yves start the race.

"Did you see him summon the beast?" Odin asks, knowing Thor was long gone, sunken at the bottom of the sea by that time. "Perhaps you should not be so self-centered, assuming you would win and taking your time," Odin says ironically, pausing to eat a bit of some food he obviously brought back with him from his meal. Thor doesn't talk back to his father; he just listens, knowing he has been beaten. "You let your ego get the best of you. Now be gone with you and learn from your mistakes." And with that, Thor vanishes. Odin sits quietly for a moment. The audience sits in silence, having just witnessed the king's anger upon Thor and not wanting to agitate him even more. They wait quietly and watch for his next move.

"It appears you have done it again, you clever Vikings," Odin turns to the children and addresses them directly. "I will not be so naive this next time."

Challenge 3: Land vs. Sky

By the third challenge, the children are learning how to pull together and use their strengths wisely, but they also know they can't get too overconfident, for that is the very downfall of the gods.

"Okay, what's next?" Yves asks, hoping Jotur and Tredge have been working on their next challenge while he was racing.

"Well, I guess it's my turn," Jotur says, letting out a sigh of nerves. "...and I know what I can do."

"What? You can't challenge them in being a smart mouth," Tredge tells her, trying to be funny. She really isn't in the mood for his jokes right now.

"Very funny, but no...," Jotur tells him as she reaches over to gather the boys closer. She leans in and begins to whisper. "Tredge, you know, we discussed it."

"Oh yeah, horses!" he admits.

"No, you can't ride one of the Valkyrie's horses!" Yves objects.

"As much fun as that sounds, no, that's not it, but close." Jotur hadn't even thought of that but reassures Yves that isn't quite the challenge. "It is clever if I do say so myself," she tells them. "Tredge, you can fill him in on what we discussed while I get us started," Jotur tells him as she steps forward to address Odin.

"Well, good luck!" Tredge tells her and gives her a little hug.

Yves is only just back from his own challenge, and now Jotur is off to compete. He looks at his sister, hoping she knows what she is doing, and smiles encouragingly.

He knows his sister is a good rider, but the challenge has to be just right. The Valkyries are excellent riders too. It has to bring out her strengths and hopefully any weaknesses of the Valkyrie, if there are any. But, he has to trust his sister because there is no time to debate.

"You got this!" Yves yells to her. He then turns to Tredge to be filled in on the details of their plan.

As Jotur begins to address Odin, she chooses her words carefully and then speaks up.

"I will challenge Brynhild, the Valkyrie leader, to a horseback race," Jotur speaks clearly and precisely. Brynhild, sitting not too far away, is excited to jump on the challenge, but Odin, seeing her reaction, puts his hand out to stop her. She takes the hint and sits back down, resisting the urge to accept the challenge immediately.

"Continue," Odin tells Jotur, now knowing to listen to the whole challenge before deciding whether to accept or not.

Jotur continues, "…But not winged horses, of course, only ground horses of our world." Jotur knows she is a good rider, but so is Brynhild, and she needs to level the playing field if she has a chance to beat her at all. Odin thinks for a moment, trying to see a flaw in the challenge or for something he might be overlooking, but he can't find anything. He then motions to Brynhild, who begins to rise, giving her the okay to accept the challenge now.

"Is that a yes or a no?" Tredge asks Yves.

"I don't know," Yves replies. "I'm hoping a yes because we don't have a backup plan." Odin begins to speak, adding clarification.

"The race will take place on natural surfaces such as grass or dirt, and may have obstacles such as hurdles or natural jumps like brush or trees in the way." Odin does not want any surprises this time. "This race will be a test of speed, stamina, and skills."

After Odin confirms the challenge, he claps his hands three times. Within minutes the two large gates leading to the arena slide open. Two identical size chestnut quarter horses enter the arena.

"They look just alike!" Yves comments.

"Well, there are two differences on their hooves," Tredge tells him, always noticing the smallest details. Odin acknowledges the caretaker and allows him to address the crowd.

The horses are both a golden chestnut color with white stripes down their noses and patches on their hooves. "These horses are twins, mirror images to be exact, perfectly matched in every aspect of speed, strength, grace, and stamina. They have been raised identically, eating the same food and getting the same type and amount of exercise. They are the pride of the stables, and they would be perfect for such a race," the caretaker informs all those listening.

Jotur can't help but admire the horses. To represent the Norse God, the saddles are decorated with an emblem of three interlocking horns. Jotur knows this symbol of triple horns is commonly worn as a sign of commitment to the Odin faith. She closely admires the horses from afar as the caretaker continues to introduce them.

"These horses are the finest in the land. The one with the white patch on his right front hoof is called Alterbar, after his father, who is strong and fearless. The horse with the patch on his left front hoof is called Leisure, after his grandfather, who is zealous and steadfast," the caretaker tells the audience, then bows his head to Odin, offering his prize horses for the race. When he lifts his head, he adds, "I took the liberty of preparing the horses. They are saddled and ready. I even added blinders to prevent them from any distractions during the race." The caretaker concludes the introductions by parading the horses around the arena, then bows again and hands the steeds over to the Viking and the Asgardian.

***

As soon as the caretaker backs away from the riders, they are transported to the center of a deserted coastal town along with their horses. It happens just as swiftly as Yves had appeared on the beach of the North shore.

As Jotur looks around at her new surroundings, trying to get her bearings and stroking the horse's nose, she hears Odin begin to speak.

"Upon the sound of thunder, the race shall begin," he says with conviction. "Follow the path to the finish line. The first horse and rider that crosses over the finish line is the winner of the race."

Thunder starts to roll as Odin finishes. Jotur knows she doesn't have long now. She gathers her two braids and puts them back with a tie she carries on her wrist, then looks over at Brynhild, standing just three feet away.

"Good luck," Jotur says to Brynhild. Brynhild ignores the Viking's gesture, not understanding what luck has to do with anything.

Two servant men take the horses by the reins and lead them toward the starting gate. The riders follow their horses toward a premade pen that is more like a three-sided box outlined in rope. *'Not very elaborate for Asgard,'* thinks Jotur. It has just enough room for each horse to walk in and turn around. When the horses are in place, there is just enough time for the riders to mount.

Jotur begins to climb on top of Alterbar but stops. Humble in her quest, Jotur knows she can't accomplish this task alone, and before Jotur mounts, she leans over close to her horse's neatly braided mane and whispers. Alterbar gently turns his ears back to listen, "You are a beautiful creature, unique and matchless. Ride with me in confidence, be steadfast, and we will win," she says, knowing it will take more than just her riding talents to beat the Valkyrie leader. It will take a skillful horse too. Alterbar raises his head high and neighs in a pledge to do just that. Jotur then takes the reins and mounts, swinging her leg over her horse. She is now ready for the race of her life, and Alterbar begins to paw at the ground in anticipation.

In the gate next to Jotur is Brynhild, preparing to mount Leisure. Brynhild is very beautiful, but Jotur knows not to be fooled by her elegance, for she is also very strong and an excellent rider. Brynhild takes a deep breath, takes the reins in her hands, and mounts Leisure.

'If Brynhild is anxious about riding a horse on land, she isn't showing it.' Jotur thinks as she watches her mount. Unbeknownst to many, Brynhild has never ridden any other horse except her own winged steed, Vladimir, nor

has she ever ridden on land before but only in the clouds. Jotur has hoped this would be the case.

Odin sits on his throne in the arena with anticipation, waiting patiently to give the signal to start the race. Standing next to his father, Thor commands the rolling clouds to climax with the grand applause of thunder. The horses jump as the thunder startles them, and the riders give them a little kick to signal them to start. Both horses shoot out past the rope and down the road into a quick gallop. Within seconds, all that can be heard are the rhythmic sounds of horses' hooves on the cobblestone streets which lay below their feet. Tredge notices, with his keen eye for detail, that Brynhild seems somewhat disturbed by the sound. As Brynhild tightens up on the reigns, seemingly in distress, Yves can see Alterbar get a nose ahead of his counterpart Leisure.

'Hmmm, this just might work,' he thinks to himself, *'but it is too soon to tell.'* The horses reach the edge of the village and quickly pass through the town's gate, and the sound of their hooves dissipates. The dirt trails silence the clopping noise, and Brynhild is back in the race. Brynhild doesn't hold herself back, and neither does Jotur. Leisure and Alterbar are even again, galloping neck and neck, darting between trees, over the bushes, and speeding down the trails, kicking up dust in their wake. This goes on for twenty minutes without Leisure or Alterbar ever breaking a sweat.

"Don't you think we need a more challenging landscape?" Odin asks Thor rhetorically, not really caring for his opinion. Before anyone can say otherwise, he waves his hand, and the two are transported to a different part of the country where the air is damp and the ground wet.

"I did say natural surfaces, correct?" Odin looks at Var to confirm, but regardless, the terrain has already been changed. "…and this is natural," he says as if to tell himself it is fair. Surprisingly, neither of the two horses breaks a stride during the transition.

"They're in Moore Land now," Tredge exclaims. "Is that fair? He just changed them without notice," he asks Yves, thinking it isn't right and worried about his sister.

"Well, do you want to question it?" Yves responds, knowing the answer.

Tredge doesn't respond. This new plane is definitely more rigorous on the horses, making it more difficult for the riders as well. The new terrain instantly changes the pace of the race as Odin had hoped it would. The horses slow as they struggle with their footing. The riders must find steady paths for their horses on the wetlands by jumping ditches and searching through high grass for safe passages. Neither one of them is leading or following anymore. When they reach the coastline, the path leads them to uncharted stretches of sand with debris and wreckage. Running in the sand takes twice the energy for the horses, and Jotur knows this.

"Just breathe," Jotur says to encourage Alterbar. "You got this."

Irritated by Jotur's optimism and Brynhild's inability to pull ahead, Odin makes one final switch from the harsh environment to an even more treacherous one, leading them right into a forest. The trail is now dark and overgrown, demanding the riders' total concentration.

Dead tree limbs covered with thick vines hang over the path, obstructing it from view. The riders must push away the growth, jump fallen limbs, duck from low-hanging ones, and carefully look for alternate routes when blocked. Jotur rides swiftly across the land of trees, holding on by the reins with both hands, with part of Alterbar's mane in her fist, a trick she learned from her father. It gives her stability and continuity as she goes with the horse's gallop. She feels as if she is moving with him with each maneuver, each step, leaping with him as he soars over the fallen trees, not against his movements, but ducking through branches and leaning as one. Leisure and Alterbar are fast, and their forms and gestures are identical, but the rider and horse have to be as one, in sync, to be successful on such a rough, unwavering course.

Tredge and Yves watch closely from above.

"This race is going to be close," Tredge says out loud to Yves, not meaning for anyone else to hear and hoping no one did. The gods' egos don't like races to be close, let alone lost.

"It's too early to tell," Yves responds, worrying about why his sister hasn't pulled ahead yet. Brynhild is slowly falling behind. She is trying to keep up, but with all the obstacles, she is not riding as smoothly as she usually does, and the horse's gate on the ground is throwing her balance off. She decides to fall back and stay close behind Jotur to follow her lead until she can see the finish line and take the lead. Brynhild sends her horse to dodge obstacles and jump when Alterbar dodges and jumps, she ducks when Jotur ducks. The strategy seems to be working, but Brynhild still rides with some uncertainty, and Leisure can sense it. The ground is hardened with dry mud underneath his hooves, making his gate rough and unsure. In some spots, the ground is very dusty. Following so closely behind Alterbar, the dust flies up and clouds Brynhild's vision. She can follow Jotur and Alterbar's lead, but not if she can't see. She is used to smooth riding, gliding with wings, not with hooves hitting the ground.

"This is not riding," she says aloud to herself, and Leisure hears her. He knows she's hesitant, which makes him uncomfortable and unsure, but he doesn't know how to calm her.

Jotur, continuing to push forward, realizes Brynhild is behind her and knows this is her chance to finally pull ahead. One last time Jotur leans in to whisper, "You're like the wind, Alterbar, you ARE the wind," she tells him. "Soar like the wind!" The words inspire Alterbar, but Brynhild is still close behind.

As the trees begin to clear, she takes off for the finish line. She can hear Leisure's hooves still close behind her. The horses' hooves are like music to her ears, and, for a moment, she closes her eyes, feeling the brisk air on her face. She forgets about her brothers, her parents, their village, and the fires that burned everything to the ground. She forgets about losing her parents and their long journey to find them. For a brief moment, Jotur is back home, riding in her pasture without a care in the world and the wind at her back.

The dream is suddenly broken by the loud sounds of horses' hooves on cobblestone streets. They are once again on the village streets where the race began. She begins to slow down, trying to see Brynhild. But she doesn't… instead, just ahead of her, stands Leisure breathing heavily. Crushed to see Brynhild's horse in front of her, not remembering him passing her, Jotur composes herself and looks for Brynhild to congratulate. However, as soon as she dismounts, she is immediately transported back into the arena. She's startled by her sudden appearance and looks around for her horse. '*No goodbye? Not even a thank you to Alterbar for running so hard? No congrats for Brynhild? I could at least meet her, you think,*' she says to herself, not realizing the impact of a lost challenge.

"Leisure has crossed the line first," Odin announces. "You have…," but before Odin can finish his announcement, Var appears and whispers to him.

"The rules state that the first horse AND RIDER to cross over the finish line is the winner of the challenge."

"And…Leisure won," Odin tells Var.

"No, actually, Leisure crossed the finish line first, but there is no sign of Brynhild," she admits to him.

Odin was not aware of what had transpired on the ground. He did not actually see the race finish, but on seeing Leisure at the finish line, he assumed Brynhild had won and was transported back to the arena immediately after the race was complete.

"Are you serious?" He asks Var, knowing she is always serious, especially when it comes to the rules. "Well, find Brynhild!" he tells her.

Odin looks up and begins to address the Vikings again, "Well, it seems as if you have won my child." He directs his comments to Jotur.

Jotur is still wondering what happened. *'Maybe something happened when my eyes were closed. And how did Brynhild leave so quickly,'* she wonders.

When the boys hear the official ruling, they run over to Jotur. When they reach her, they both grab her up in a group hug.

"What happened?" she says to them.

"What do you mean? You won the race!" Yves says to her, not understanding why she isn't more excited.

"One minute I was racing, and the next I'm here, and it's over," she explains to Tredge and Yves, who look at her, wanting more of a reaction to her win.

"Let's move on to our next challenge!" Odin says, rushing the children.

Jotur, still trying to compose herself, leans over toward Yves' ear. "Someone doesn't seem pleased," she says.

"Obviously, Odin wants to move on," Yves tells her.

"Yeah, he doesn't want any whispering about it," Tredge says.

"Whispering about what?" Jotur asks, still looking for an answer to what happened at the end of her race. "Yves, tell her," Tredge says.

"Well, you were ahead of Brynhild but not necessarily Leisure," Yves whispers in Jotur's ear so as not to irritate Odin by talking about it.

"What? That doesn't make sense; you're talking in riddles," she tells Yves, wishing he would just spit it out.

"She fell!" Tredge says.

"Who fell?" Jotur asks in astonishment.

"Brynhild!" Tredge and Yves say simultaneously.

"Brynhild fell?" Jotur asks.

"Yes!" they both answer together again.

"You kind of won on a technicality," Tredge tells her. "Leisure won the race, but Brynhild wasn't on him."

"Seriously?" she asks. "Why didn't I notice that?"

"Did you have your eyes closed or something?" Tredge jokes.

Jotur doesn't answer. She is beginning to feel guilty. She had a hunch Brynhild would have trouble riding on the ground. And Odin kind of confirmed her suspicion by switching up the terrain. Jotur had guessed Brynhild wouldn't be used to the gate of a horse but never thought she would fall off. She didn't want her to be hurt or embarrassed or not even finish the race! Jotur is declared the winner, but she doesn't feel as good about it knowing the truth now, but it was their lives on the line.

"Children!" Odin says, irritated, "As I said, next challenge!"

Challenge 4: Beauty is more than Skin Deep

The Asgardians' hearts are beginning to turn, and the crowd is starting to cheer on the little Vikings openly. They are impressed with the children's determination, cleverness, and love for their parents. Naturally, Odin doesn't take a liking to this new attitude.

"Okay, okay, quiet down," Odin barks to the crowd. "So you have earned your lives back, but now you will fight for your parents and Ultor." He blatantly questions to rattle and unnerve them. "Do you think your luck will hold out? You will eventually have to choose one life, maybe two to stay...you still have two challenges left," Odin tells the children, hoping they will begin to worry about such a feat that they won't be able to think straight, let alone be clever enough to come up with two more challenges.

"Lose our parents?" Tredge asks his siblings, falling victim to Odin's bantering.

"He's right. What will we do if we lose our parents after all this?" Yves says, playing into Odin's hands too. "And what is he talking about choosing?" Yves asks, wondering to himself, *'If the three challenges won our lives back, then are these last two for our parents and Ultor? Do our parents count as one? Will we have to choose?'*

"Well, at least we know Ultor wants to go to Valhalla when he dies. I bet he would be okay with us choosing him to stay," Tredge adds optimistically.

"No one is staying, at least not yet," Yves assures them. "Not even Ultor!" It isn't clear to him which challenge is for which life, but he doesn't want to know and doesn't care to find out.

"We can't concentrate on that right now," Jotur says, trying to refocus the group. "Now it's Tredge's turn to compete again. I hope you two have something in mind; now, what is it?" she asks.

"Well, it's a little silly," Yves says.

Tredge laughs out loud, "You could say that again!"

Jotur, not amused by her brothers, asks again, "What is it?"

"Okay, you need to think outside the box for this one...I think Tredge should challenge the daughter of Freya to a contest."

"Who?" Jotur asks, confused. "If my memory serves me right, isn't she the most beautiful Asgardian of the land? Challenger her to what?" she asks. "Oh, I don't think I want to know!" she exclaims nervously.

Before they have time to explain, Odin calls out. "Your next challenge!" Odin demands.

"No time to rest?" Jotur, now composed, leans over to whisper in Yves' ear. "Someone doesn't seem pleased," she says.

"I don't think we are winning him over," Tredge comments.

"Apparently not," Yves responds, noticing the same annoyed tone in Odin's voice. "But I think we are winning over the crowd!" he replies with a smile and motions for Tredge to step forward. "…And that is just what we need for this next challenge," Yves tells them as Tredge steps forward.

"Now say exactly what we practiced," Yves tells him. Tredge just gives him a thumbs up and takes his place in front of Odin.

"I would like to challenge Hnoss," Tredge says loudly so as not to be misunderstood, maybe a little too loudly, but he is not misunderstood.

"What can you possibly challenge her to?" Odin replies, looking puzzled. "She is the fairest and most beautiful Asgardian of the land. You can't hold up to her beauty." Odin motions for Hnoss to come forth. Hnoss enters the throne area where Odin sits and curtseys as she takes her place next to him. Odin smiles at her beauty. As Tredge watches Hnoss approach Odin, his worries are put to rest, and he turns to Yves and winks.

"I'm not a fighter or a swimmer or a rider, so what is it that you could possibly challenge me to?" Hnoss asks. "Please explain," she says to the littlest Viking standing before them.

"Yes, please explain," Odin asks. He is curious about how they could challenge such an alluring goddess. Enjoying Hnoss' presence and being taken by her beauty, Odin almost agrees to the challenge without hearing what the Vikings had in mind.

"I want to challenge Hnoss to a funny face-making contest and allow the crowd to be the judge," Tredge answers. He and Yves thought bringing the Asgardian spectators into the competition as judges would please Odin and ensure his approval to challenge Hnoss.

"Very well then," Odin agrees, definitely liking the idea of the Asgardians being the judges. "Hnoss, do you agree to take on this challenge with this young Viking boy?" Odin asks.

"Of course, it will be fun," she answers in a sweet soft voice.

"Okay," Odin says, smiling in delight. "Whoever can make the people laugh the most by making a funny face wins. You will each get three turns," he says in a booming voice. *'Simple enough,'* Odin thinks to himself, *'but why do they want to challenge Hnoss?'* he wonders.

"Hnoss, can you join the boy in the arena?" Odin asks politely, and she nods. As she begins to step down into the arena to join Tredge, all eyes are upon her. The crowd has grown immensely since the Viking's first challenge, and with her graceful presence, all chattering stops. Yves even stares at her.

"She is beautiful," Jotur says, agreeing with the books that dubbed her more beautiful than the gardens of the gods, but it isn't just her outward beauty that is intriguing. Hnoss carries herself with such poise and gracefulness, and there is a pleasant disposition about her as if nothing harsh or unkind could ever come out of her mouth. After seeing Hnoss in person, Jotur and Yves can understand why she is referred to as the most beautiful goddess in all of Asgard.

"You could say that again," Yves replies to Jotur, not taking his eyes off the goddess yet.

Watching Hnoss with pride, Odin speaks up, "Hnoss, you will go second," thinking it will help her get some ideas from her opponent. Tredge, knowing he needs to have everyone's full attention, steps up and places himself right in front of Hnoss. Luckily for him, he is already a little funny looking. He has two front teeth missing, and his face is as round as an orange.

Tredge thinks for a moment, then turns his back to the crowd for a more surprising effect. He then turns back around with his lower lip sucked into his mouth through the gap of his missing teeth and pulls his big ears out to the sides. A few giggles flare up, but not the reaction he was hoping for, so he turns back around. Tredge then takes a deep breath, and while turning a bit red, he bugs his eyes out from their sockets like two golf balls, a trick he used to use in school to startle the little Vikings. When he turns around, laughter erupts with this look, but it is still not enough to win the challenge, and Hnoss hasn't even gone yet.

'*Okay, last chance,*' he thinks as he turns away from the crowd one last time. '*This needs to be good.*' Tredge then crosses his hands under his helmet, which is too big to begin with and lets his fingers hang down like thick strands of hair over his face. He turns around on his tiptoes like a ballerina. Everyone laughs at his creativity. Tredge sticks out his tongue like a dog licking his nose, hunches over, and pretends to walk with a limp, but then unexpectedly falls, truthfully unintentionally, and the crowd roars. Even Odin chuckles, almost indiscernible, but a chuckle nonetheless. Tredge loves the attention. With that, he turns to Hnoss and bows to give her the stage.

Hnoss steps forward and smiles shyly; she thinks for a moment, then tries to cross her eyes and look at her nose, giving a crooked smile, but no one laughs, so she sticks out her tongue too. When she stops, she looks out among the crowd, and there is no response. The audience watching her is still waiting for a funny face. Hnoss then tries to use Tredge's trick and turns away from the crowd for a surprise attack. When she turns around, trying to make her best funny face, the crowd sits there still waiting. The more she pouts her lips, makes her eyebrows move or tries to mess up her hair, the more beautiful she looks.

Tredge, starting to laugh at her lack of ability to make faces, stops himself by looking away. He thought she wouldn't be that good at making faces when they came up with the plan, but he can't believe how she really has no idea what she is doing. Hnoss takes another deep breath and tries one last time. She begins by pulling her ears up and forward, sticking her tongue on her upper lip, and making a noise like a monkey. It is adorable. The harder she tries, the angrier she gets and the cuter she looks. Tredge, not necessarily trying to mock her, makes his monkey face with his tongue and ears, and the crowd roars. As everyone bursts into laughter, Odin knows the little Vikings have won their fourth challenge.

Challenge 5: Wits or Follies

Yves is laughing out loud at Tredge when Jotur grabs his arm.

"Hey, we didn't plan another challenge!" Jotur tells Yves, beginning to panic. "I was so busy watching Tredge, and he won so fast. What are we going to do?" she asks.

"I know exactly what to do," Yves answers. "Watching Tredge gave me an idea."

"But have you thought it out?" she asks. "Are you sure? You have to be sure! You have to be smart." she tells him, not having a single idea of her own.

"Yes, that is precisely what I have to be for this challenge...smart!" he says to her playfully, though she doesn't quite understand what he means.

"Well, you know he is going to ask for the next challenge soon," Jotur says to Yves as she snaps her fingers at Tredge, trying to get his attention.

"Yeah, I know," Yves agrees, knowing well that Odin doesn't like to wait. "Do you think he would let us take a break?"

Jotur laughs. "Aaghhh, no!"

"I'm tired," Tredge admits to Yves and Jotur as he finally joins them. "Making faces is exhausting; my cheeks hurt!"

"Yeah, and I'm a little hungry," Yves confesses.

"Yeah, making people laugh makes me hungry too," Tredge agrees.

"You're always hungry," Jotur teases him. But the boys are right. They don't have the stamina of the gods. And it is getting late, or so she thinks, by how long they have been out there. She doesn't know if Asgard goes by time or if the sun ever sets, but their bodies do, and it is starting to feel like dinner time. Odin abruptly shouts.

"We need to start the next challenge. I will propose one if you cannot think of another," Odin suggests. Of course, that is the last thing the Vikings want. But they have taken up more of the god's time than he intended, and he is growing impatient. Yves, however, already has their next challenge in mind, but they are stalling to rest.

"We will have one in just a minute," retorts Jotur as nicely as she can, trying to hide her own irritation, but seeing Odin's displeasure in her tone and perceived lack of respect, she quickly counters. "I mean, can we please have just a minute?" He nods, allowing them one more minute.

"I have the next challenge," Yves admits. "And I know exactly what I can do, trust me," he says, reassuring his siblings.

"But will you at least tell us who you are going to challenge?" Jotur asks.

"Hoenir," he tells them and steps forward to address Odin.

"Hoenir? I could challenge him! He's not the brightest god," Tredge whispers to Jotur as they watch Yves take his place to speak.

"Shhhh, don't let them hear you say that!" she scolds him hoping no one heard him. "Let's just hope Yves has thought this through."

Yves clears his throat and begins to address Odin and the crowd. "We are ready for the fifth and final challenge."

"Well, let's hear it; it's about time," Odin snaps.

Yves proposes the final challenge. "A mere Viking can't outwit an Asgardian, let alone a god. I challenge Hoenir to a game of wits."

Odin thinks for a moment, then speaks up. "Whoever gets the most correct answers wins the challenge." Odin agrees, presuming that the children couldn't possibly know more than a god. "Wits it is! Three questions each," he adds and calls forth his son Hoenir. Hoenir is a very handsome god. The books describe him as having hair as dark as night, eyes as blue as the skies above, and the complexion of perfection. Odin is quite proud of his son. The spectators watch as Hoenir walks toward the Viking children and takes his place in the arena.

"Hoenir is to ask the first question," Odin states, and the children nod their heads in agreement, not about to argue.

"Fair enough," Yves replies.

Hoenir steps forward and takes his place in front, and Yves begins to follow his queue, but just before he steps to join him, Jotur whispers to him, "He may speak well, be charming and handsome but remember, he isn't as witty as you," she reminds him lovingly. Yves smiles back, appreciating her attempt at encouragement. Yves then steps forward to begin. Hoenir turns to Yves and faces him to ask the first question.

Yves begins to gather his thoughts and compose himself. *'To come so far and lose the last challenge, after all we have been through, would be dreadful,'* he thinks, *'But it is what it is,'* he whispers to himself.

"Are you ready?" Hoenir asks the little Viking. When Hoenir speaks, the crowd listens intently to his deep, masculine voice. Jotur can see Yves begin to doubt himself. Hoenir is very intimidating, though he is not purposely trying to be so, but she doesn't think he would try to trick Yves. Like his father, he is likely arrogant, thinking a Viking couldn't possibly know more about the gods than an actual god, and trickery wouldn't be necessary.

"Yes, sir, go ahead," Yves answers respectfully. "Does that count as a question? I know I got that one right!" he adds, trying to relieve some of his own anxiety. A simple look of disapproval from Odin answers his question, and Yves quickly shuts up. Hoenir begins.

"In all of Asgard, who is the greatest soldier?" Hoenir asks loud and clear.

After hearing Hoenir's first question, Yves is put to ease a bit and answers quickly, without a doubt, "Your brother, Tyr." Hoenir shakes his head in agreement, but Yves can't let it go at that, and he continues, "...and Tyr has only one hand, but he is still the greatest soldier of all time."

"Don't show off book worm, just answer the questions!" Jotur, standing just a few feet behind, whispers to him.

"But it is the correct answer nonetheless," Yves whispers back. '*Okay, my turn,*' Yves thinks. He already has several questions picked out but can only ask three of them. He is still trying to narrow them down, but selects his best guess to stump the god, stands straight up, and faces Hoenir.

"Whose death will indicate the beginning of Ragnarok?" he says clearly and loudly for all to hear. A few in the crowd look puzzled, and whispers start amongst them for the answer.

"Silence!" Odin says, quieting the spectators.

Yves knew it would stump some, '*but will it stump Hoenir?*' he wonders. Hoenir takes the forefront and begins to answer.

"Balder, one of my brothers," he replies. "That is an easy question." Apparently, Hoenir is brighter than the Vikings expected, though he is a god after all, just not the cleverest god.

"Maybe Yves underestimated him," Tredge says to Jotur.

"Let's hope not," she tells him and quickly puts it out of her mind.

"There is no other way. We must win," Tredge interjects. "Come on, Yves! You got this. Think, think!" he shouts to Yves.

Hoenir takes no time to prepare for his next question.

"What are the names of Odin's two wolves?" Hoenir asks, thinking it will definitely stump the little Viking.

This is a clever question. Yves now has two answers to get wrong, two questions in one. *'Very clever, Hoenir. Why didn't I think of doing that?'* Yves thinks to himself. If he gets one name wrong, the whole answer is incorrect. But Yves knows the answer without a doubt, and in a matter of seconds, he responds with his answer without giving it much thought.

"One is named Freki, and the other is, the other is...." His mind goes blank. But he knows this answer. His dad would tell stories about them, and he saw them in Valhalla on Odin's throne! But nothing is coming to mind.

"Seriously, Yves, now you freeze!" Jotur speaks up.

"Quiet!" Odin immediately barks at her.

"Freki and Gaki," he answers quickly.

The crowd sighs at his answer though Odin looks pleased. "Freki is correct," says Odin, "but the other is Geri, not Gaki, incorrect answer!" adding a grin.

"Rats!" Tredge says. "I knew that one. Yves taught me!"

"Your turn," Odin says, pleased that the gods are winning now.

Yves understands this is it, and he has to stump Hoenir with a difficult question, but what? Finally, he thinks of one to which he doesn't even know the answer. The ultimate puzzle.

"How can Thor's hammer, Mjolnir, be destroyed?" he says with a cunning smile because there is no correct answer. Hoenir is stumped.

"It can't be destroyed," he replies.

"Surely it can be destroyed," Yves says, "...and you just don't know how."

"I will accept Hoenir's answer," Odin jumps in, taking advantage of the unanswered question. Yves was hoping Hoenir's omission of not knowing how the hammer could be destroyed would be an easy win, but his idea backfired. Instead, Hoenir gets the point, and it is his turn to ask the next question.

"Who is Ymir"? Hoenir asks quickly to throw Yves off.

"Ymir is a giant from which Odin and his brothers, Ve and Vili, made the world," Yves says confidently.

"Correct," confirms Hoenir.

"Ask your third and final question," Odin tells Yves.

Yves takes a deep breath, holding on to hope that they can still come out on top. "If Asgard and Bifrost are not to be found by mortals," Yves begins, pausing to make sure he asks the questions correctly, "then how were we able to find them?"

Hoenir drops his head in defeat, for he knows that he cannot possibly know how the Vikings found Bifrost, let alone Asgard. Seeing the expression on his face, Yves knows he doesn't know the answer. If Hoenir answers that he doesn't know, Yves is afraid Odin will rule his response as correct, for the gods really didn't know how the little Vikings entered Valhalla. So he needs Hoenir to guess at an answer for it to be obviously incorrect. Jotur and Tredge walk over to Yves to stand by him, hoping the challenge is over.

Making one last attempt, Hoenir speaks, "A map?"

Yves simply answers, "No."

"I don't know then, it should be impossible for mere mortals to find us, but somehow you did," Hoenir says, baffled. "I yield."

Tredge and Jotur hug Yves, squeezing him tight.

"Okay, okay, I have to breathe," he tells them.

"I can't believe it. You did it!" Jotur says.

"What do you mean you can't believe it," Yves says, looking at her with confusion. "I thought you believed in me," he teases.

"Sure I do, but he is a god, you know," she says as she can't stop smiling.

"The contest is over!" Odin interrupts their premature celebration. "You have won your lives, but you lost the last challenge."

"But I thought we won the challenges," Jotur speaks up. "You said we couldn't LOSE a challenge, and technically we didn't lose any challenge."

"No, you won four challenges and tied one challenge," Odin reminds her. "That is a LOSS for you."

"But a tie is not a loss, and we are competing against gods!" she rebuts.

"Hoenir and Yves both missed an answer, so it is a tie," Odin argues.

"A tie isn't a loss," she repeats. They were hoping this was the end of the challenges and they could finally see their parents. And finally, go home.

"The deal is that you win five challenges," Odin rebuts. "…and you didn't win five challenges." Odin then asks Var for her ruling if a tie is a win or a loss. The two gods bow their heads towards each other to contemplate in private. The whole arena waits on bated breath for the ruling. After a few minutes of deliberation Odin speaks again. Yves, Jotur, and Tredge watch in anticipation of the verdict.

"You must still win one more challenge," Odin says, not pleased with the ruling. "I will choose."

"Ahem," Var clears her throat and leans in to speak with Odin privately again. After a few more minutes, Odin speaks.

"You will select your next challenge," Odin says, correcting his first statement.

"Of course, he can't just let us have a tie!" Tredge says, not surprised.

"Your next challenge?" Odin asks, giving them no time to discuss a challenge.

Yves, Jotur, and Tredge stand again at a loss. The boys look at each other and then to their sister, who just stares blankly ahead. Jotur had a fleeting thought of a sure-win challenge when Yves was asking his questions, but she didn't bring it up. She was sure they wouldn't need another challenge, sure Yves would outwit Hoenir. She is afraid to say it out loud. She knows the boys will not like it, but they will definitely win.

The Last Challenge: Family Ties

As the three young Vikings stand in a huddle, hopefully for the last time, win or lose, Jotur, having pushed her emotions away for as long as she could, can no longer help but express her feelings towards her brothers.

"Tredge, I am so proud of you and how brave you have been," she says, holding back tears. "...And Yves, your courage and wit to take on the gods! I am proud of both of you. We have carried this burden together as a family, and each has pulled their weight, demonstrating their strengths. I only hope Mom and Dad are here somewhere watching," Jotur tells them with a bit of sadness in her voice. Yves and Tredge know the day has been a little emotional but don't understand why she is beginning to unravel now, with only one challenge left.

"Wait, so do you think we are going to lose the next challenge?" Yves asks.

"Yeah, because this is beginning to sound like a loser's speech," Tredge tells her.

"No, but...," she stutters. She meant to inspire them, not discourage them.

"But what?" Yves asks, wanting to know what she is thinking.

"Yeah, but what?" Tredge repeats after him.

"I have the next challenge, and we will win," she tells them confidently. "...and I believe we have proven ourselves to the gods of Asgard that we are worthy of being heard."

"This next challenge better be a sure thing," Yves stresses. "A winner."

"It is," she says. "I promise you we will win, and it will guarantee your safety and the safe return of our parents and Ultor." Jotur doesn't tell the boys of her plan for fear they will reject it, and she steps forward. Her brothers start after her.

"No, trust me, it's a sure win for us," Jotur admits waving for them to stay back. Then, without looking either one of them in the eyes, she addresses Odin.

"Wait, Jotur, tell us first!" Yves is afraid of her plan. *'Why isn't she consulting with us, at least?'* He realizes she didn't mention her name in the "guaranteed safety" speech. His heart begins to sink in fear. *'What is she about to do?'* he asks himself.

Jotur ignores Yves' plea and speaks. "I challenge Balder to a contest to see who can be most easily wounded," she says, choosing her words wisely.

"What?" Tredge asks, looking at Yves for answers.

"NOOOO!" Yves shouts.

A hush falls over the audience when they hear the name Balder. Jotur can hear the gods in the crowd murmuring to each other, "Balder, did she say Balder?"

"Yes, each to take only one arrow shot at them," she continues. Those who were only half listening suddenly turn their heads to pay closer attention. All know the legend of Balder and how he is one of the greatest warriors who can't be wounded.

"Let me get this correct, young lady; you want to fight Balder?" Odin asks, confused.

Even Loki asks for clarification, "Did you say Balder?" amazed by the children's boldness. He snickers at the idea, *'Clever,'* he thinks, *'very clever young Vikings,'* and a grin comes over his face. Loki imagines the possible outcome of the proposed challenge but, keeping his predictions to himself, takes his seat to watch the drama unfold. He is all about the drama.

"Balder? Well, that's just outlandish!" Freya cries out. "If he is wounded, it will signal the beginning of Ragnarok, the end of the world."

"But Balder has never had even one scratch on him," Thor reminds her.

Then, as if Odin is trying to distract the Viking children, he signals to a guard. At that moment, Ultor is released from his holdings alongside the arena. Perhaps it is a tactic to persuade them to give up and shake some sense into the children. Or perhaps it is for him to say goodbye. Whatever the reason, the elder Ultor walks slowly into the arena; though Tredge and Yves don't walk, they run when they see him. They didn't know he was so close, watching them all this time.

"It's nice to see a familiar, or should I say a friendly face around here!" Yves says as he gives him a big bear hug.

"I thought they would surely kill you!" Tredge doesn't hesitate, grabs his leg, and doesn't let go.

"I'm so proud of you three," he tells them. "I can't believe what you have done, you are so brave, and I'm so blessed you pulled me out of that rubble and saved me." He waves his hands as if to erase all the gripes and grumbles he made that day. "I'm so glad I'm here today to witness this day the children Vikings triumph over the gods."

"Shush, don't say that so loud," Jotur tells him as she walks toward Ultor with her arms stretched out for a big overdue hug.

"Yeah, the gods have some pretty big egos," Yves says bluntly, "and with those egos...."

"...comes big hot heads!" Tredge interrupts.

"Well, not exactly what I was going to say, but basically, yeah," Yves whispers to the others. "Eg-os self-esteem-os erupt-os." He chuckles at his play on words as if it is some unbreakable code.

"If I had died in the ashes of the village," Ultor looks at Jotur and turns serious,

"I might have already been in Asgard, but I would have missed the opportunity of knowing you, each of you," he says in a sentimental tone. "And though I would have still seen you fight today, it would not have had the same meaning as it has had today. I believe my destiny was to travel with you and to help you to reach Asgard," Ultor tells them as he fights off the tears, trying to put on a brave Viking face. He knows the challenge Jotur is suggesting is very dangerous. He knows what she is about to do for the sake of the family.

"Are you sure you know what you are doing?" Ultor nonetheless has to ask her. "The gods use Balder daily for target practice with their bows and arrows."

Tredge's mouth drops open. Now he is afraid. He didn't understand the seriousness of the challenge, but after seeing the fear in Ultor's face, he is scared for Jotur and begins to worry. Tredge looks at Yves for reassurance.

"Trust me, I know," Jotur assures them, looking at Ultor. "This last challenge will end this once and for all. Not even a tie is possible!"

Ultor knows the children well enough by now to know they had a plan. But he doesn't know that Jotur hasn't clued Yves or Tredge into it yet.

"I do, child, I do trust you," he says, leaning over to kiss Jotur on the forehead. With that encouragement, he lets Jotur take the lead once again. Now, realizing that Jotur could acquire serious injuries during this challenge, the crowd starts to ask questions.

"So she's willing to sacrifice herself for her family?" one god could be heard asking.

"She'll be sacrificing her life for her parents, her family!" another god says, answering the first.

"She's willing to give the ultimate sacrifice to win their lives," one goddess exclaims.

"Could she die?" another asks, seeming genuinely concerned for Jotur. "Who would return home with her brothers if she dies?"

"…but what about her?"

"…how will she survive?"

Questions and answers are flying around the arena from the groups gathered there—gods, goddesses, Asgardians, dwarfs, and giants, creatures that Jotur had thought to be only myths until a few days ago, all whispering, concerned for her life and the lives of her family. Finally, Jotur begins to speak, ignoring the conversations in the stands. The assembly of gods quiets down immediately to listen.

"Each of us, Balder and I, will be shot with one arrow. Yves will shoot both of the arrows," she holds up an arrow to demonstrate and continues, "…and whoever suffers the greatest wound wins." Loki is very impressed with Jotur's ingenuity and watches intensely.

She lowers her hand, and as she does, her eyes meet Yves', unintentionally. He now understands what he has to do and what she is asking. Inside he is trying to suppress his own fears, but he shows her none. He must show her complete confidence.

"Yves, you have to shoot me," she says after their eyes have met. Jotur knows this will work, but Yves is hesitant. She can feel it. She has complete confidence in her brother's ability and has calculated every angle and possible outcome. *'This must work,'* she tells herself. *'... but there is still no room for error.'* Jotur gives Yves her bow and quiver of arrows as everyone now watches gravely. There is a bit of edginess in the air. For the first time since the challenges began, the little Vikings actually feel like the gods don't want them to lose.

As Yves takes the bow, he thinks that he has never before been more afraid of shooting an arrow. Jotur begins to take her place for the challenge, looking at Tredge, who has already started to cry, as she makes her way to the center of the arena and positions herself as a human target, twenty paces away from Yves. Tredge looks on, petrified. His sister has become like a second mother to him since their mother and father were taken by the Valkyries.

"Please, Jotur! Please!" Tredge cries out to her one last time, but she stops him by holding up her hand and mouths, *"I love you forever and always, trust me,"* and then blows him a kiss. Tredge jumps to catch it and shoots her one back with an invisible bow and arrow as their parents often did.

Jotur turns to Yves and says, "Yves, you have to shoot me here," as she points to her ribs.

The crowd is watching without a sound—no more whispers or muttering to break the silence. After the results of the previous challenges, they are wondering what the three little Vikings are up to. They now know they cannot assume anything. Jotur looks at Yves again.

"Yves, you have to shoot me right here," she repeats as she points to her ribs.

"Well, if you say so, I thought you'd never ask." Yves plays light of a very heavy situation.

"Yves!" Tredge yells, giving a very disapproving look at his humor. Yves points right at her shoulder.

"No, here," she reaffirms the same spot as before. "I'll be okay."

Yves begins to set up and then stops. "What if I get nervous and miss the spot?" he asks her. "I couldn't live with myself if…." The pressure is getting to him. All eyes are upon him. The toughest Viking of the three starts to fight back the tears. "What if I freeze again?" he asks, not wanting to do this.

"There is no other way," Jotur reassures him. "Trust me. You're the best," she says one last time, "…and are you really turning down a chance to shoot me?"

"Shut up!" Yves tells her. "You know I really do love you."

"Yeah, I know," she says as she smiles faintly, then turns to face him, waiting.

"You're the best sister I've ever had, Jotur," he says as he begins the setup again, trying not to tear up. *'Be brave for them,'* he tells himself.

"Aaghhh, I'm your only sister," she says, putting her feet together, standing tall and straight.

"Stop it! We know she will be hurt," someone in the crowd breaks the silence, "and Balder will be untouched by an arrow. Let them win!"

"PROCEED!" commands Odin, upset with the disturbance. He must stand by his word, five challenges.

He cannot waiver. If the children want victory, they will have to earn it. Very focused on the task at hand and not distracted by the interruption, Yves doesn't move.

"Now, don't breathe," Yves says. "This is going to bite a little."

"Seriously, just shoot me and get it over with before I wimp out!" Jotur says. Yves draws back the bow very slowly and precisely. He aims and fires. The minutes seem to stand still as the arrow flies through the air toward Jotur. The crowd, gods, Vikings, and even Odin are spellbound, watching every second as the arrow moves in slow motion closer and closer to Jotur. When it finally hits her, the crowd responds greatly, not with cheers but gasps as she takes it. It has flown straight into the exact spot Jotur had pointed at earlier. The shot is perfect. The arrow sinks deep into her right side. The tip of the arrow has gone all the way through her and is sticking out of her back. She crumples over and sinks down almost immediately, but before she hits the ground, Yves is there by her side to catch her. She groans and begins to lose consciousness from the pain.

"I'm sorry, I'm sorry, I'm sorry!" Yves whispers as she falls unconscious.

Tredge just watches as tears flow down his cheeks. He walks to his sister's side to hold her hand. "I'm here, Jotur," he tells her.

"Boy, continue," Odin shouts without sympathy, though there is plenty from the on-lookers. Yves gently lays his sister down, placing her head in Tredge's lap and his hand on her wound to help with the bleeding, showing Tredge what to do. He wipes the tears from his face and walks into the open arena to face Balder. Balder, who had quietly watched all this unfold, steps up.

In his deep gruff voice, he grunts to Yves, "Now you shoot me. Do so quickly so that your sister can be saved, and this contest shall be over." He takes his place twenty paces away from Yves. "Do not fear to hurt me, for I cannot be harmed," he assures Yves. "She is very brave, your sister," Balder tells him.

Yves lifts his bow and aims straight at Balder. He makes the shot just as straight and forceful as always, but the arrow just breaks and falls to the ground leaving no scratches on Balder. Yves immediately rushes back to his sister's side and kneels beside Tredge, still holding Jotur's head in his lap. Balder turns and speaks.

"These brave Vikings have won the contest," declares Balder as he looks over at Odin. "Quickly, bring Eis, the goddess of healing, so that she might tend to this child."

The goddess appears and reassures Yves and Tredge that she can heal Jotur and that their sister will live. Eis gracefully kneels beside Jotur, puts one hand in hers to comfort her, and gently but swiftly breaks the end of the arrow off and pulls it out. Jotur gasps loudly with the rush of pain, squeezing Eis' hand tight. Eis looks into her eyes and says nothing, but her look of love and compassion comforts Jotur. She relaxes a little, easing her grip on Eis' hand. The goddess then places both of her hands over the wound.

"It's bleeding; she's bleeding a lot," Tredge says as he pulls on Yves' clothes to get his attention. He is scared;

they are both scared. But Yves barely blinks, refusing to take his eyes off his sister.

"Shush, just wait," he waves him off, annoyed at the break of silence as if it would disturb the goddess. Suddenly the goddess leans forward, kisses Jotur's' cheek, and rises. "What, that's it? That can't be it? Isn't there something else you can do?" he says as he falls to his knees in front of the goddess.

"Yvveeesss," Jotur says. He looks back over at her from just a few feet away and stares, frozen for a moment in denial.

"I'm here, I'm right here," he says to comfort her, snapping back to life as he takes his place beside her. He reaches out to take her hand, but before he can even grasp it, she pulls it away, using it to brace herself on, and sits up. Jotur looks a little confused but nonetheless conscious and alive. Remembering bits and pieces, she gazes down at herself, looking for the arrow, a wound, something. She reaches and puts her hand on the very spot where she remembers getting shot by the arrow.

'Strangely enough, I don't feel any pain,' she thinks, and she can't find where she was hit. She looks around her side on the right, but she can't see a wound. She examines her left side, front, and back. Then, reaching back around to the original spot, she finds a tear in her vest. Placing her fingers through the hole, she notices blood on her clothing.

"Am I bleeding?" she asks. "I don't feel anything." She begins to look across her chest, her shoulder, and down her arms, but she can't find any fresh blood or even a gaping wound from the arrow. All evidence is gone except for the dried blood on her garment.

"Was it a dream?" she asks Yves again for answers, but he is speechless. Yves is happy to see Jotur is okay, but all he can do is muster up a smile. He almost lost his sister, and that frightens him. Tredge wants to embrace her, to tell her how much he loves her and how crazy and stupid she is for suggesting such a feat, but he doesn't, he stays back and watches, frozen.

Balder walks over and helps Jotur to her feet, showing everyone–Yves, Tredge, and the rest of the crowd, who also watch in silence–that she is completely healed. Balder tries to explain to her what happened after she was shot by the arrow. She just looks at him, staring at his grandeur. Jotur has never actually seen Balder before, only pictures in a book. Before, she wasn't sure if he was a myth or reality, but here he is, standing in front of her, talking to her, telling her she was shot by an arrow.

Balder then leans down to her and whispers, "I don't think you understand. You won, you won the challenge, all the challenges!"

"Silence!" Odin bellows loudly. He is upset, knowing the three little Vikings have beaten him. The children are afraid they have angered the gods, angered Odin, the ruler of gods, but what choice did they have but to fight? Yves, now standing next to his sister, looks at Tredge. He still hasn't spoken to her. None of the children make a move. Jotur takes Tredge's hand hanging beside him to show him she is okay. Yves finally breaks his silence.

"What's going to happen now?" he asks his sister as if she knows.

"I don't know. Where's Mom and Dad?" she asks. Of course, they had all been wondering that throughout the day's events.

"We just wait and listen, I guess," Yves says to his siblings, turning to look at the front of the arena where the king of the gods sits on his throne. Odin looks mad. The three Vikings stand there, waiting, fearful of what Odin might do next. Loki leans into his father's ear, reminding him that he is a wise and fair king. As disappointed as he is at the defeat, Odin knows he must honor the agreement. He addresses the children.

"It is rare indeed that the gods of Asgard would celebrate their own defeat, but today these Vikings have shown bravery, the purity of love, and loyalty to family and us all," he says, gesturing with his hands toward the young Vikings and motioning to the crowd.

"Come, and celebrate with us in The Great Hall for your victory." Odin smiles for the first time as he addresses the Vikings. "Everyone, come celebrate the champions," he announces, and the crowd cheers with his generosity. The children's eyes widen with surprise at such a gesture.

"Did I just see a smile?" Jotur asks aloud. "I think I did!" she says, answering herself as she turns to hug her brothers. Tredge jumps in Jotur's arms.

"Easy there," Yves reminds Tredge.

"No, I'm okay. It's okay," she says, planting a big kiss on Tredge's cheek. Tredge reaches up to his cheek and begins to rub it.

"Don't rub it off!" she tells Tredge.

"No, I'm not! I'm rubbing it in," he replies. "Hey, do you think they'll have cake? Or strawberries? I love strawberries!" Yves and Jotur laugh at their brother's sweet innocence and youth. For the first time in days, the Viking children feel a lightness return to their spirits.

"You're the guests of honor; I'm sure they will have all sorts of things you like!" A voice says coming from behind. Tredge jumps down from his sister's arms and runs over to Ultor. As the four begin walking together, escorted by guards, they finally get a real chance to talk.

"Did you see everything? Did you see me?" Tredge asks excitedly. "I beat the gods!"

"Yes, I saw you. You were brave!" Ultor laughs at Tredge's expressions. "I think you'll have some stories of your own to tell now," he gives Yves and Jotur a big hug. "I'm so proud of you, all of you," he whispers to them as Tredge continues to talk.

"I sure will!" Tredge replies. "I can tell you how the dwarfs didn't carve ANYTHING and how big Balder really is in person! And...," Tredge continues telling him all about the gods and Yves' race across the sea and Jotur's horse's name as they are escorted out of the arena. Ultor doesn't have the heart to remind Tredge that he saw everything from his place in the stands. He just listens, happy to be reunited with the children again and with all their struggles behind them.

CHAPTER V

DEPARTURE FROM VALHALLA

The Great Hall of Valhalla is the first place in which the Valkyries would bring their selected heroes that died on the battlefields. However, today the Vikings are not being brought to the Hall of Valhalla because they lost their lives or to live out their afterlife, but for a banquet for heroes. It is here where their parents would have been brought right after their village was destroyed, and the children know this, hoping they will still be there, waiting.

Before reaching the Hall, a group of guards, Ultor, and the young Vikings are led through a garden that leads to the main entrance of The Great Hall of Valhalla. The garden is woven with intricate details of green ivy and plant life, and flowing through is a river of vibrant colors with flowers such as soft white water-lilies and jasmine of grace and elegance. There are no actual doors on the outlying building adjoining the hall, only open corridors with tall marble columns with gold leaf accents marking the entrances.

"I bet we are the first uninvited guests to step foot into the garden," Yves says to the group.

"Yeah, and probably the last uninvited guests!" Tredge adds.

Upon entering the gardens of Valhalla, they are sure they are the first of their kind to venture into such a noble establishment alive. The three Viking children, with the elder Ultor, are taken to a room where they are allowed to clean up before heading to the banquet hall. The servants hand them warm wet towels to wash their hands and faces.

"What are these for?" Tredge asks the others.

"To wash off all those faces you made," Ultor says with a laugh.

"Yeah, we don't want everyone looking at you and laughing at dinner, now, do we?" Yves teases him too.

"Tredge, don't listen to them," Jotur says as she gives Yves and Ultor a stern look and walks over to Tredge. He doesn't mind it, though. He likes the attention, even if it is teasing. Jotur takes him by the hand and leads him over to a bowl and pitcher to help clean him up.

"However, you are a bit dusty," she says sweetly as she begins to clean his face. The others take the hint and start to clean off the dust from the arena left on them. The hot water and towels help them to feel refreshed, but not Jotur.

Tredge, standing next to her, comments, "You smell like a horse."

"I think your right," she replies, not knowing what else she could do. The water alone doesn't do the trick.

"Okay for dinner at home, but not for a banquet with gods, don't you agree, Tredge?" she says. He nods.

The ladies assisting the Vikings overhear the children talking and excuse themselves, only to come back a few minutes later with fresh clothes for each of them. Jotur is escorted to an adjoining room with the sweet scent of flowers to change. On the dresser, she finds a fragrance bottle with the aroma of jasmine to her liking. Soon the four are back together, looking much more presentable than they were before, standing under the arches outside that mark their path.

"I can honestly say, in this case, pictures don't say a thousand words!" Jotur says, "…and we aren't even inside the hall yet! I can't imagine what it is going to look like," she adds.

"Yeah, the pictures in the books at home left out a few details," Tredge points out quite loudly.

Yves agrees, "Yeah, The archives will definitely have to be updated in the Thor Tower! They just don't do this place justice now, do they?" he says in agreement without taking his eyes off the elegant entrance. With each step closer, they are further immersed in its grandeur.

"You can say that again!" Ultor says as he follows Jotur, Tredge, and Yves into the corridor.

"The pictures in the books…," Tredge starts to say again.

"Tredge!" Jotur interrupts to stop him.

Once past the garden and grand entrance, the Great Hall was just that, A Great Hall. Tredge pulls on Jotur's arm, "Look, look up!" he says, pointing at the white sheer-like curtains hanging from the ceiling.

She can see that familiar look of mischief in Tredge's eyes and warns him, "Don't you even think about it!" Jotur almost shouts at him after having a vision of Tredge pulling the whole lot of them down on top of everyone. "You'll pull them down," she tells him, calming her voice to a more stern but still sweet sound.

"Yes, they do look like fun," Yves says, encouraging his brother and looking to get a reaction out of Jotur. She rolls her eyes at him, but she, too, can't resist reaching out her hand as she passes one of the draperies and running her fingers through the silky-smooth edges allowing them to pass swiftly through them.

"They're so soft and delicate," she whispers. "They feel like silk, but even softer. They are almost ethereal."

"Look over there," Ultor says, pointing off into the distance ahead. He is just trying to distract Tredge, who looks like he is wondering if the drapes could hold him.

"Cool!" they hear Tredge exclaim as he runs ahead. "Look at the rafters. They are shaped like spears!"

"He notices everything," Jotur says to the others. They follow Tredge as if he knows where they are going.

"Yeah, maybe he should be the one to update the archives when we return," Ultor replies.

"This place is beautiful," Jotur whispers again.

"I'm sure the gods know their kingdom is beautiful, so why are you whispering?" Yves teases.

"I don't know, perhaps to be respectful, maybe we aren't supposed to be loud in here or something," she replies.

"It's not sacred ground," Yves says, laughing at her.

"Look at the floors!" shouts Tredge.

"He isn't shy about expressing his emotions out loud," Yves points out.

"They look like crystal marbles all swirled up," Tredge continues.

Yves joins in, "…and the ceiling, the light blue is like the ocean or an endless sky on a summer day."

"Yves, must you encourage him?" Jotur asks, but she's starting to laugh a little too.

They are definitely impressed with the Great Hall of Valhalla. So much so that they don't see all the eyes of the many gods standing in the corridors staring at them. Once inside, the four are led up the royal staircase by two guards. The staircase is adorned with mother of pearl with oak steps and leads immediately into the banquet hall. The little Vikings stop at the landing and gaze upon the Gala below, appreciating the view.

"Ultor, look!" Tredge points out another grand structure to him as the old man lags behind, finding the stairs a bit tiresome for his age.

"I see, Tredge, very impressive," Ultor replies when he reaches the top. The children still do not notice the gods surrounding them, but Ultor looks up at one of them and smiles. The gods seem humored by the children's love for life and excitement.

"It's breathtaking," Jotur sighs as she tries to absorb every detail from the candlestick chandeliers, which give off soft, radiant light. The adornments of delicate white lilies add to the oddity of the hall's roof of shields with various crosses and colors. "This is a sight that will be forever etched in my mind," she says to the others.

The banquet hall is adorned with glass doors leading to balconies on either side, which overlook all of Asgard. Seen from the balconies are the borders of Asgard east, west, and north. There are symbols of gods, history, and trophies in every direction. Jotur tries to see everything and memorize every detail. She doesn't want to forget this when she returns home. As she draws nearer to the banquet area, she hears Tredge.

"This is awesome!" Tredge shares his sister's sentiments but more in reference to the abundance of food that garnishes the dining tables. The tables are already set, the décor is in place, the chandeliers are lit, and all is prepared and perfect.

'But how is all this possible?' she says to herself. Then she remembers she is in Asgard, after all.

The Feast

Per Odin's orders, following the challenges' conclusion, a great feast is prepared for the children and other important guests to attend. The banquet hall is decorated with three themes to represent the day's event: bravery, loyalty, and love. These are explained by Frigg, who met them at the table prepared for them.

"Congratulations, young Vikings. I am so pleased to finally meet you," she says, kindly greeting them. The children bow shyly as they aren't sure of the proper greeting to the wife of Odin but know their gesture would demonstrate respect.

"To represent bravery and strength, the hall is decorated with Steel Bladed Swords," Frigg says as she points toward the head table in the front of the room.

"Stunning," Jotur remarks as she looks closer at the three swords placed carefully, one across the other, upon the table.

"The three shiny metallic swords are laid to represent each of you brave Vikings," Frigg continues. "To represent loyalty and friendship, the color turquoise is chosen, often seen as a color of good fortune," she tells them. The three Vikings look around in awe at the banquet hall adorned with silk ribbons of turquoise blue and steel gray. The tables and chairs are also decorated with simple elegance.

"In addition, there are baskets of fresh strawberries and white lilies to represent love," Frigg says as she picks up one of the baskets placed sporadically around the tables. The flowers leave a scent of spring-like fragrance in the air.

"I hear you like strawberries?" she asks, offering one to Tredge.

"Yes, mam!" he answers as he takes one from the basket.

"Tredge!" Jotur scolds him.

"No, it's perfectly fine. This is all for you," Frigg smiles, motioning around the Great Hall, and encourages Tredge to take another as he does so obligingly. No sooner than the strawberry is eaten, Tredge starts to run toward the large table full of food. Embarrassed by his lack of restraint, Jotur quickly grabs him and yanks him back.

"Patience, Tredge, what are you doing? We are still among the gods. Show some respect, walk and be patient!" She obviously does not see what he is seeing. Tredge, held tightly by Jotur, is twisting to get loose from her grasp then he finally shouts.

"Jotur, let me go! I want to see Mom!" Puzzled by his words, she looks up and breaks her hold on her brother. Looking in the direction Tredge is running, she now notices what he is trying to tell her. There, at the head table, just as beautiful as she remembers, are Sigvard and Elsa, healthy, unchanged, and alive. Both of them are beaming with pride for their brave little Vikings. Elsa smiles and stands up from the table, stretching her arms out in front of her. Tredge runs into his mother's arms while Sigvard leans over and hugs him.

"I am so proud of you," Sigvard says. "You have grown too!"

"Yeah, a whole tomme!" Tredge says, excited his father notices he has grown an inch.

"Well, maybe more, but close enough," his dad chuckles.

Jotur and Yves try not to run but walk very quickly with a bit of grace, which turns into a little jog before they reach their parents. The family embraces for the first time since that dreadful day when they last saw one another in the burning courtyard of Svalbard.

The children leap into their mother's arms. "I will never take these hugs for granted again," Elsa says as she squeezes them.

"Boy, you have gained weight too," Sigvard says as he throws Tredge into the air.

"I ate all my meat," Tredge tells his dad proudly.

"I am so proud of you, of all of you!" Sigvard tells the children as he gives Jotur and Yves a great big hug.

"Did you see me? Did you see me, Dad?" Tredge asks.

"Yes, every one of you!" Sigvard confesses.

"I held my breath the whole time! I was so very nervous," Elsa admits.

Sigvard looks down the table, and there sits Ultor. "It seems that you kids have put your faith in the right place," he tells them, grateful for their trust in Ultor.

Jotur, Yves, and Tredge all look down at Ultor resting at the end of the table and wave to him. The children finally notice the many faces that surround them.

"Jotur, look!" Tredge says as he begins to notice the gods who have filled the room.

"There are many Asgardians here to greet you," Jotur says. "The boy who beat the amazing dwarfs!" she teases.

All the citizens of Asgard in the hall watch the Vikings' joyful reunion with genuine warmth and admiration. The gods gather around the tables, beginning to take their seats surrounding the children and their parents.

"This is thrilling," Hymir, the giant, says childlike with excitement. "We have guests, we never have guests, and children, how exhilarating."

"Can you believe that a little Viking raced against the mighty Thor?" Loki says, trying to stir up trouble, always up to something. Loki is quite proud of today's scheme and how everything turned out.

"Outwitted Thor is more like it," Hoenir replies. A few of the brothers chuckle at the thought of it.

"Sheer poetry," Bragi replies.

"Yeah, they got you too, Hoenir," Loki smirks. "You thought you were too clever to be outwitted."

"I have to admit that face-making contest was genius, though," Balder says, trying to copy Tredge's facial expressions and failing miserably. "Who would have ever thought of that as a contest?"

"Viking children, "the goddess Eis speaks. "My brothers are quite amused, for we have never lost, let alone to mortals. They mean you no harm," Eis reassures the Vikings they are safe now from the gods as they listen to the conversation.

Thor pulls up a chair next to Sigvard and Elsa and sits down at the table, casually joining the conversation, saying, "Yeah, historically, gods win the challenges."

"Well, you especially, Thor," Elsa replies shyly.

"If you had asked me yesterday, I would have said it was a foolish thought to think you could beat a god in a challenge, let alone more than one," Thor says.

"Your children are quite courageous," the goddess Var says, smiling at both Sigvard and Elsa. And with that said, she bows her head in respect and steps back, retreating for others to greet the parents of the brave Viking children.

"Yeah, I hope it doesn't give the other mortals any ideas!" Thor says, still sitting with Sigvard and Elsa.

At that moment, two more sons of Odin appear, Balder, the god of light, and Hodr, the god of night.

They walk toward the banquet table where Tredge, Yves, and Jotur are sitting.

Tredge, recognizing them, nudges his brother to look up. "Yves, look!" he says, pointing at them as they walk across the room. Yves looks in awe. This whole experience still seems like a dream, and they will wake up tomorrow back home in their village as the same young Vikings, none the different.

"Here come Balder and Hodr to greet you," Thor says as if he is informally introducing them.

"His eyes are so blue," Jotur whispers dreamily to her mother as Balder and Hodr walk toward the table. Elsa just laughs at her daughter's bluntness. She has never seen her daughter take a liking to any male, let alone a god. Hodr is Balder's twin, and though you can't tell by looking, he is blind. So Hodr lets Balder speak first.

"On behalf of all the sons of Odin, we would like to present you with this token of our respect," Balder says, standing in front of the table. The three children stand up and approach Balder and his brother. Yves bows to the gods, Jotur curtseys, and Tredge, taking the hint, bows too.

Hodr speaks up, "The front of the amulet we have presented you is adorned with the cross shield surrounded by the Elder Futhark."

Ultor, who is now seated at the head table, whispers to Yves, "That's the runic alphabet, which may be of use someday."

Pretending not to hear Ultor's remark Hodr continues, "This symbol is awarded to you today for your bravery and provides you protection." He pauses, and the two gods begin to place a pendant around each of the children's necks. Hodr then continues again, "It also symbolizes each of Odin's nine virtues: courage, honesty, honor, truth, strength, hospitality, industriousness, self-reliance, and perseverance." Tredge lifts his pendant up and takes a good look at the symbol and its intricate detail.

"Cool!" he says, not noticing that everyone is still watching and listening. They all smile at his sweet innocence.

"Shhhh," Yves nudges him.

"Sorry," Tredge respectfully bows his head.

After slipping the pendants over Jotur's and Tredge's heads, Balder speaks again. "The inscription on the back reads, *'Unharmed go forth, unharmed return, unharmed safe home.'*"

Being the eldest, Jotur speaks up. "I speak for my brothers and myself when I say we are grateful for your gifts and your kindness," she says, curtseying again. "We could have never expected such a warm welcome and greatly appreciate your hospitality." And with that said, Hodr and Balder take a step back, bow to the Vikings, and turn to walk away. Tredge, Jotur, and Yves can't believe their eyes. The gods just bowed to them.

"In addition, the amulet is strung on a lanyard of turquoise beads in remembrance of the theme shown here today, symbolizing friendship and loyalty, and sterling silver chains, symbolizing strength and bravery," Frigg reminds them. Just as Yves, Tredge, and Jotur return to their seats, Thor speaks.

"Let's toast," Thor says as he stands up from the table and lifts his glass.

The children grab a glass from the table to join in on the toast. All who have gathered raise a glass toward Odin, who is sitting at the end of the table watching the festivities. The gods always held their glasses toward Odin, who would take the first sip showing his approval of any toast proposed.

"To the Vikings who's bravery and insanity," the gods chuckle at Thor's good humor, "with no magic, or magical flying creatures," he points at Jotur, "...we are thoroughly impressed and are glad that your victory is not without merit. We celebrate you!" he says, raising his glass and waiting for Odin's approval. But, instead of taking a sip, Odin sits up in his chair and begins to speak himself.

"Success occurred here today because these three Vikings showed courage, perseverance, and love. They came here with one purpose, one objective, one goal, and they are not going home without it, am I right?" The children smile and shake their heads in agreement but do not interrupt.

"We all have said this today, and I will say it again, they have demonstrated great courage. It takes courage to stand up in front of gods, in front of me, and ask for something, let alone to challenge me!" The assembled group nods in agreement. "I have heard that Vikings were courageous creatures, and it was surely demonstrated here today. Your countrymen should be proud." Odin looks over at the children and gives what some may consider a smile.

"…And perseverance, this attribute surprises me. I really thought you would not last, nor would I see so much determination in three little children not to give up. I wish I could see this kind of diligence in my own children!" Odin puts his glass out to be filled, still not taking a sip, having the crowd wait in anticipation for his approval of the toast.

Odin continues, "And last and probably most importantly, they came here out of love. Love for their parents and for each other is the basis of their actions, and it is the reason they felt completely justified in their deeds." And with that sentiment, Odin raises his glass, takes a sip, and the audience cheers and drinks to the toast for the three little Vikings from Svalbard. As Odin lowers his glass, he adds one last thought, "These are attributes that would benefit all the gods to learn."

The Journey Home

The feast lasts for what seems like days; however, it is all put to rest in just a few hours. It is almost springtime back in Svalbard now, and Elsa is anxious to get home to see her flower beds, feel the warmth of the morning sun through her kitchen window, and see what is sprouting in the garden she loves so much.

"I bet the gardens will need a lot of work when I get home," Elsa says to Sigvard as they walk toward the gate of Asgard with their children and Ultor following close behind them.

"Yeah, and I better not hear you complaining," Sigvard jokes.

"Never again!" Elsa says, leaning over and putting her arm through his. A crowd begins to gather.

"Are they here to see us?" Tredge speaks up as he runs to his parents and joins them. The others begin to take notice too.

"Not us, to see you, Yves, and Jotur!" his mother tells him, smiling. She is very proud of her children and their bravery.

"To see the mighty Viking children who challenged the gods and lived to tell about it!" Sigvard says, giving him a wink. Before too long, the Vikings are surrounded by dwarfs, giants, and gods. Asgardians from all over have gathered, lining up on both sides of them, leaving just a narrow pathway for them to walk through, leading them to the gate. The goddess Vör steps forward from the crowd, stopping the three little Vikings in their tracks.

"With this token of the olive tree, I give you wisdom wherever you may go to do all things righteous in accordance with the gods." She leans forward and sticks a pin onto each of their coats. Tredge, learning to watch and take his brother's and sister's queue, watches Yves and Jotur for their response.

"Thank you," Yves says as he bows his head in respect.

"We can't thank you enough for your generous gift and will treasure it always," Jotur says as she curtseys and bows her head simultaneously.

"Ag, you," Tredge looks at Vör, losing his train of thought, and that's all he can get out of his mouth. The crowd giggles at his sweet gesture.

"What's the matter there, kid?" Yves teases, "I've never seen you tongue-tied before." Tredge's face begins to turn red. But quickly, the attention is turned to others who want to wish them well too. With Vör's gesture, it seems as if all others are given the okay to approach the Vikings. Emiter, the goddess of agriculture, harvest, and nourishment, and Idunna, the goddess who keeps the apples of youth, both walk up to Elsa and Sigvard with food, apples, and fruits and vegetables for their trip home.

"Stay healthy on your journey," Emiter tells their mother. As Elsa reaches out her hand and takes the provisions, she smiles at their generosity. Sigvard quickly takes them from Elsa to carry them for her.

"Godspeed," Idunna says as she hands over a basket of apples.

"Thank you for your kindness," Elsa respectfully bows her head, as does Sigvard.

The tokens of affection continue as they seep ever closer to their exit. They are provided blankets by Holda, the *gracious one* as she is called, lanterns from the god of light, Aether, and water from Nerthus, the goddess of the lake and springs. When they finally reach the gate of Asgard, the king of gods approaches them for the last time.

"The gifts you have received from the gods are no ordinary gifts. They are eternal and will sustain you on your journey home and wherever future journeys may take you," Odin says. "Go steadfast and strong as we will all be watching." And with those few parting words, he motions for his guards.

Tredge thinks to himself, *'Soon, the gates will open, and we will finally be going home with our parents.'* But, to his surprise, instead of the gates opening, the crowd parts, and six horses emerge. Tredge's mouth drops open, and Jotur's heart begins to race.

"Godspeed," Thor says, smiling at Tredge, and hands the reins of the smallest quarter horse in the group to him. "His name is Sleipner, and he will be good to you."

Tredge, beside himself, can't control his excitement anymore. "Mom, Dad, can I keep him? Is he mine? Wow! This is so cool!" he says as he begins to mount the horse.

Jotur, having become quite the little mother, quickly corrects him, "Manners Tredge, don't you have something to say?"

"Oh yes. Thank you! Thank you! Thank you! Can I keep him?" Tredge asks as he is now sitting on top of the horse.

"Of course, he is yours," Thor replies.

Jotur, feeling the same excitement as Tredge but keeping it on the inside, quickly eyes Alterbar and can't hold it anymore. She quickly runs over and caresses the stallion.

"I never thought I would see you again," she says to the horse.

"He is yours," Thor tells her.

"But...I can't...I couldn't," she says hesitantly.

He simply replies, "You two ride as one and belong together."

"I can't thank you enough," she tells Thor, grabbing him and giving him a big hug.

He is taken aback by the Viking's affection, and she realizes she has just hugged a god without permission and jumps back.

Thor laughs and tells her, "You are the finest rider on land, and a great rider needs a great horse."

"I will love him forever!" Jotur declares.

Yves, his eyes on the white horse in the group with a tail and mane the color of golden honey, walks over and scratches him behind the ears. "I guess it's you and me," he tells the horse. "What's his name?" he asks, rubbing his soft mane.

"That one is called Knight," Thor tells Yves.

"Perfect," Yves replies.

"...and those are Nash, Giles, and San," Thor says, introducing the remaining horses and pointing to each. The others walk up to a horse, thank him for his generosity, and quickly begin to load up their supplies upon the horses.

Sigvard turns before mounting, "I appreciate all you have done for my family to ensure our safe return home. We will be forever in your debt." And after a quick bow to the god of thunder, he mounts Nash. With that queue, Ultor and Elsa mount Giles and San. Ultor, the elder, who has been quiet up until now, finally speaks out.

"Oh, Great Odin, what will become of me? May I enter Valhalla to serve in your army?" he asks.

"Ultor," Odin says in his authoritative way. "The children won the competitions; therefore, their reward and yours is to return home with their parents. Those were the conditions that were agreed upon." Odin pauses for a moment as Ultor waits, hoping for another response, but it isn't the case. "The punishment, if the challenges were lost, was to remain in Valhalla. Was this not so Var?" he asks though he knows it is true. Var agrees that those were the terms of the agreement, and so Ultor must return with the children. As Ultor walks to the gate, he takes one last look at the great city of Asgard and then never looks back again.

As the Vikings move through the gate and ride forward to the rainbow bridge, it seems like it has been years since they crossed it, just days ago. Down the way, they see Heimdall waving at them to stop. He comes up to them, panting a bit, just to tell them a secret. When he catches his breath, he speaks.

"As you travel down Bifrost, think of the place you wish to go, and the bridge will magically take you there."

"Wow, that's so cool!" says Tredge.

"Like a rainbow?" Jotur asks.

"Exactly, rainbows appear all over the world, and so the rainbow bridge can take you anywhere you would like to go," Heimdall reaffirms. "Just try it."

Tredge, of course, has to ask a question. "So we start here and think of home, then step off the other end of the bridge, and we are home?"

"Yes," Heimdall says simply to Tredge, holding out his hand to shake as a promise. Yves is amazed at the simplicity and pure genius.

"Too bad we couldn't have thought of Asgard and the bridge appear at home," Tredge says. "It would have made our journey much faster."

"But what would have been the fun in that?" Heimdall replies. "The journey is part of the fun."

Tredge agrees. He has learned so much on the journey itself. The children wave Heimdall goodbye, and he seems delighted with their kind-heartedness. The Vikings bid their horses forward and begin to head toward home, thinking of Svalbard.

"Hey, we were all thinking of home anyway. Would it have taken us there even if we didn't know its secret?" asks Tredge. He is always asking questions to clarify things.

"I don't know. I'm just glad we know it now," Jotur says just to please him. "Now think of home!"

"Maybe that is how we found Asgard! We were searching for it. We were all thinking of it when we stumbled into the bridge earlier. So maybe that is why we ended up there in the first place," Tredge questions.

"Out of the mouth of a child," Jotur laughs. "Maybe you've answered your own question."

Ultor, however, doesn't want to think of home. There is nothing there for him; no one left, none of his friends are living, all were either fallen soldiers or dead by now, and his family is gone, children and grandchildren moved away. He longs to stay in Valhalla, in Asgard.

Ultor rides slowly behind the others, lingering, putting off the inevitable of returning to Svalbard. The return from Asgard past Heimdall castle seems much shorter than before, especially since he knows all he has to do is think of the little village from which they came, and it would be before them. He knows the life that awaits him there. He is too old to fight, to die with integrity and honor, or sacrifice his life for the greater good. And he knows he can't even try to fight and die in a battle just with the hopes he will make it to Asgard again. He is to live out his life as it has been fated, and it becomes more of a reality with each step he takes toward home.

As the children ride alongside their parents, telling them all about their journey to Asgard, it sounds surreal.

"…And we met the whale named Brodnak and the Greenlanders," Yves tells them.

"Yeah, we even ate with them, and they were really nice, not barbaric like I thought they would be," Tredge says surprisingly. "And we saved a mama ox and her calf from wolves!"

"Wow! Wolves, whales, Greenlanders, I can't wait to get home, and you tell me everything," their dad says, encouraging them to tell him more. Elsa is actually a bit frightened that they took such a journey putting themselves in danger, but she is grateful her family has made it through together.

"What's that smell?" Jotur asks, tilting her head up and taking a sniff. The family of Vikings stops. The horses' legs buckle beneath them.

Walking a few steps ahead of the group, Yves gets the scent even stronger. "Burnt hair!" he shouts.

A pack of wolves suddenly leaps upon the middle of the bridge to keep the Vikings from passing. The Vikings immediately take heed as they recognize them as the same wolves they had fought in Greenland. Leaping from his frightened horse, Yves quickly draws his sword. "Stand back!" he yells.

The leader of the pack is covered in singed fur and angry for it. Without thinking twice, Ultor races up to protect the children. He runs swiftly to the front of the group, grabbing Yves and pushing him back behind him. The large leader from the front of the pack is now in a face-off with Ultor.

"I can help!" Yves screams.

"Me too," Jotur says as she reaches behind her, grabs her bow, and takes aim.

"No, this is my fight," Ultor yells as he jumps at the wolf. They struggle and thrash about until not one, but both fall over the edge of the bridge.

"NNOOOOOOO!" Tredge screams, and he runs over to the edge and looks below. They both have fallen into the mist below and have disappeared from sight. The remaining wolves, now at a standoff with Yves' sword and Jotur's bow, suffering the loss of their leader, back away slowly, still keeping their snouts facing the Vikings. As the pack of wolves looks forward at the two Vikings ready to fight, they forget to watch their backs and do not see what is coming from behind. Brynhild and a host of Valkyries fly up from below on their winged steeds and cast the wolves from the bridge. And just like that, the threat is gone. Elsa runs and takes Tredge up in her arms.

"But what about Ultor?" he asks.

"I'm sorry, my son," she says with compassion.

"What do you mean?" he looks confused.

Suddenly Brynhild reappears in front of them from the mist below, carrying the elder, the Viking, a great warrior and friend, Ultor. As Brynhild flies towards Valhalla, she looks down at Ultor.

"Now for your bravery, your sacrifice, you shall enter Valhalla." Knowing this is what Ultor wanted more than anything, the children cheer with excitement. Tredge, Jotur, and Yves look on, waving, as he fades into the distance, still smiling and waving back at them. This time they look on not in fright or fear, not of mourning or sadness, for they know this is right. Ultor is where he should be, among the greatest warriors.

EPILOGUE

The Jurgenson family continues to move along the bridge and walk steadily downward. The haze is gone, and the end of Bifrost looks different from when they first found the passage just a few days ago. As the bridge becomes steeper the farther down they descend, they begin to see a familiar place. And then, just as promised, they step off the passage onto the ground back in Svalbard. They are back in the village town where the nightmare had all begun. There they stand once again in front of the ceremonial hall. The village isn't abandoned as they had thought. There are Vikings who survived the raid of the trolls. The families that hid and left the village are all back to help restore the town to its former beauty.

As they re-enter the city, they dismount their horses and begin to lead them. The villagers look up at them with excitement and come to greet them. The town smells alive once again with the scent of freshly baked bread and wildflowers. The town center, the epicenter, once again echoes with footsteps and the sound of horses' hooves on the cobblestone streets. Tredge rubs his eyes in disbelief.

"Home," Yves whispers. Tears are beginning to form in his eyes.

'He's more sentimental than he lets on,' Jotur thinks to herself as she looks over at her brother. "I never thought I would see it again, let alone see it so alive with people again!" Jotur says to the boys, her eyes filling with tears too. She grabs Tredge's hand, but he quickly pulls it back.

"I'm not a child anymore," he says, looking at her seriously. He pauses, then smiles brightly up at her.

Jotur smiles back at her youngest brother. "That you're not," she says. "That you're not." The three little Vikings laugh together. And with that, the family of five walks toward home.